Spell-Kissed

Spell-Kissed

Kari Thomas

Black Lyon Publishing, LLC

SPELL-KISSED
Copyright © 2010 by KARI THOMAS

Our books may be ordered through your local bookstore or by visiting the publisher:

www.BlackLyonPublishing.com

Black Lyon Publishing, LLC
PO Box 567
Baker City, OR 97814

This is a work of fiction. All of the characters, names, events, organizations and conversations in this novel are either the products of the author's vivid imagination or are used in a fictitious way for the purposes of this story.

ISBN-10:   1-934912-28-X
ISBN-13:   978-1-934912-28-7
Library of Congress Control Number: 2010928021

Written, published and printed in
the United States of America.

Cover Illustration by Nick Phelan.

Black Lyon Paranormal Romance

I believe in Magic. The Magic in Life. The Magic in Miracles. The Magic in Love and Friendship. One of the most magical moments in my life was when my dear friend and sister, Linda Rudd, came into my life forty years ago. She brought sunshine, laughter, and endearing sisterly love. This book is dedicated to you, Sis. Thank you, always, for keeping magic in my life. Your support means a lot to me.

Prologue

"I have found the door. Nothing can stop me from gaining my soul's desire now. There will be completion."

Completion. How many countless centuries, millenniums even, had he waited for the finality of his quest? Even he had lost count.

But now his journey neared its end. He was ready to dredge up every precious ounce of the hard-won patience that had brought him thus far. *Just a while longer. And it is done.*

For one brief moment he allowed the exhilarating emotion of jubilation to rise up inside of him. The rush was heady, drugging. He reached up and pushed back the heavy cowl from his head, lifted his face to the night sky and breathed deep. The bright light from the full moon above shone down on him, highlighting his craggy features with a silver glow that appeared eerie and unnatural. His wide mouth split into a menacing grin as he stared up at the moon as though it was an enemy he was confronting. He raised his fist.

"Do you hear me?" He shouted the words into the night, hearing them echo back as they circled the small enclosed glen. "There will be completion. Completion!"

He stood in silence then, relishing the uneasy fear that masked the surrounding area. Satisfaction swelled from deep within. Then with one last look around he covered his head again, pulling the cloak's cowl low over his features.

The lilting beauty of Gaelic sounded guttural and harsh coming from his lips as he uttered the concealing spell. Moments later, his solid form faded and he walked from the glen. To the naked eye he had simply disappeared.

But to the witch concealed in spell-shadow as she sat on the boulder yards away, his aura was visible enough for her to watch the direction he went. She floated slowly to the ground. Heart heavy, fear beating at her with a ferocious rage, she went in the opposite direction.

Chapter One

He'd seen enough death to last him a lifetime. "Burned out and in danger of becoming a statistic," was what the department psychiatrist stated. Hunter Dallas grunted under his breath. Hell. He was only thirty, with less than ten years under his belt as a homicide detective. He was too young to be burned out already.

Yet, here he was facing death for the second time this hellish week and knowing—with a certainty deep inside him—that he couldn't stand much more. Burned out just didn't define what he was feeling right now. His gut clenched, bile rising to his throat. No matter how many times he faced it, it never got easier. *Damn. They were just kids.* He moved aside for the city coroner to kneel down and examine the two bodies. Or what was left of the bodies. The perpetrator—now known as the Slasher—hadn't left much after taking a hatchet to the two teens.

"Same M.O. as the last three," his partner Jamison said as he came up to stand next to Hunter. "If we don't catch this bastard soon, we won't have any teens left in the city."

"Any forensics reports yet?" Hunter asked, swallowing back the bile and clearing his throat. He was bone tired and sick to his soul with all the death. Even worse, a rage boiled deep inside him that threatened to consume him if he let go just once. He couldn't afford to lose control.

"No," Jamison replied, disgust tinting his hard tone. "Nothing much to find in all this blood. Same scene. No clues left behind. Just blood and gore. Damn it all to hell."

Hunter's thorough gaze roamed over the small alley again. He was an expert in finding clues no one else could, and he knew there had to be something someone had inadvertently missed. Killers always left behind a clue. He'd be damned if he walked out of here this time without something that would lead him to this evil bastard.

"Dallas," another cop hollered out, "Chief wants you in, now."

Damn. Who had told Rolly he was out here? "Tell him I'm on my way," he muttered back. *When I'm done here.*

"Chief says 'now, as in yesterday.'"

Rolly was already preparing to have his head for being out here tonight. Hunter swore under his breath and turned his back on the cop. "Jamison, cover for me. Tell him I left minutes ago. I need to check the area one last time."

He saw his partner hesitate, but then nod his head. They'd been friends for years and watched each other's backs. Despite the fact that Hunter wasn't supposed to be on this case now, Jamison wouldn't rat him out. Hunter retraced his earlier steps and started meticulously studying the ground and area for missed clues. He resolutely ignored the bone tiredness swamping him; it was more mental than physical and that he could handle. Later.

Hours later, exhausted and sick to his stomach, Hunter reluctantly admitted defeat. When he turned to leave the alley, he found the Chief of Police, Adam Rolly, waiting at the curb. Great. There was no way of getting out of this one this time.

"I gave you direct orders to cease on all cases and take a break, Dallas," Rolly stated in a hard tone. A bear of a man, he could intimidate even the toughest man with just a look. "What the hell are you doing here?"

"Doing my job," Hunter snarled. He didn't have time for this. But he forced himself to take a calming breath, and then exhaled. "Sorry, Chief." No sense pushing his luck any further.

"Sorry, my ass. You're the most defiant detective I have, Dallas. And sometimes that's not a good trait. What's it going to take to make you obey an order? Throw your butt in jail?"

Hunter couldn't explain it. Despite the mental sickness that was becoming so much a part of him lately, he still couldn't just walk away from a case. Any case. He had to stop the deaths. "I'll take a break when we get that bastard," he stated. "You need me, Chief."

"I need you ... sane. Hell, Dallas, you're so close to breaking now it isn't funny."

"Don't exaggerate," Hunter muttered. Even though he knew

Rolly was right. He'd seen the signs before on others and knew he was walking a thin line.

Rolly raised his brows, giving him his 'did-you-just-defy-me' look. "I'm going to ignore that remark." He opened his patrol car door. "Get in. I'm taking you home. Then, I'm officially taking you off the payroll. If you can't take that 'ordered' leave of absence, then I'm forcing you into it. I'm officially firing you, Hunter. When you're rested—later—and the psychiatrist can clear you of all potential problems, then I'll re-hire you."

Hunter spit out a few foul expletives. Rage built again, deep inside him, but with iron control willpower he managed to push it back down. How the hell was he supposed to survive a forced leave? This was his life. He wasn't a quitter. He stopped short of telling the chief what he could do with his forced leave, and got in the car, slamming the door closed.

Hours later, he collapsed on the sofa in his apartment living room. Two hours of a hard, pushing-to-the-limits workout and the rage still simmered deep in him.

When the phone rang he thought about ignoring it. But the chance that maybe Rolly had reconsidered his decision made him grab it on the second ring.

"Yeah?"

"Hey bro," his younger brother Sloan answered back. "You sound angry. What's up?"

Hunter grunted. "Long story. How are things in your neck of the woods? Mom doing okay?"

"She's fine," Sloan said, then chuckled. "She has a new pet project and it's keeping her busy. Don't ask. It's too crazy." He sobered. "The reason I'm calling is because I need your help. We've got a—uh, weird—case here, and I haven't had the time to really investigate. I could use a second pair of eyes to help me find clues."

Hunter frowned, his voice hard as he muttered, "Damn. Rolly called you, didn't he."

There was a moment of obvious hesitation before Sloan answered. "Yeah, he did. He's concerned about you, Hunter. And frankly, after what he told me, I'm worried too. You need a break, bro. A long break. And knowing you, you're not going to take it without a fight. Since I have this odd case, I thought it might be a good time for you to come visit, help out, and still get some much needed R and R." He chuckled. "And keep you out of range of Rolly's radar."

Hunter ran a hand through his hair. Indecision warred inside him. On one hand, he didn't want to walk away from the 'Slasher' case. On the other hand, he knew he'd have a harder time trying to work it if every damn man in the department tried to keep him out of things.

And ... he *was* burned out. Too many deaths. Too many nightmares from the failures.

He sighed, hard, his heart heavy. "I'll catch the next flight out," he told Sloan. Maybe, just maybe, he could find a way to regain what he'd lost: The belief in humanity ... and in himself.

Chapter Two

She really didn't need the salmon, but at this point every little bit helped. In her business the salmon represented wisdom, and Goddess knew, any amount of that certainly wouldn't hurt.

Witch Briana Adair remained frozen where she hid in the shadows of the large bush yards from the back door of the novelty shop. Thank the Goddess for a moonless night. She felt relatively invisible in the head to toes, black, skin-tight cat-burglar outfit she was wearing. But no sense in taking chances so she stayed in the concealing shadows, scurrying from bush to bush until she reached her destination. She'd already struck this place once before when she'd "borrowed" the large antique copper pot displayed in the front window. She was counting on the chance that the police wouldn't expect another theft at the same location.

She grimaced. Okay, so it was in fact a theft—but she preferred to call it borrowing. She had every intention of returning the items as soon as she was finished with the spell. She could have easily bought the needed items, but the persistent feeling that her enemy was closely watching her every move forced her to resort to other methods in order to stay under his radar. 'He' couldn't know ahead of time what she was planning.

Mentally she went over her list of necessary instruments. She had the copper pot, copper utensils, smudge stick and incense, rosemary and yarrow plants from the local nursery, and was about to grab the copper salmon plaque. That left the rare doves from the local zoo. She stifled a giggle. *That's not going to be a fun heist.* If things weren't so desperate right now, then this whole situation would have been a big laugh.

But, it was desperate. Seriously, life-altering, world-saving, desperate. And it was all her fault. She had been the Guardian of the Sphere ... and she'd lost it. Granted, she hadn't purposely lost it. One moment it had been there in her possession and then the next moment it had disappeared. Poof! Transported away in the blink of an eye. The invisible thief had struck quickly—leaving no traces behind.

Horrified, shocked, frantic, she'd immediately started uttering spells to locate it. If she'd only thought—rationally—before acting then she wouldn't be in this precarious position now.

She was a witch with one disastrous fault: when her emotions were out of control so was her magic. Her spells would go awry in the oddest ways, sometimes comical and sometimes seriously problematic. To her chagrin, the most disastrous results came when she was emotionally ... aroused. She tried to avoid that state at all times. There wasn't anything worse than turning your date into a toad or ... something else.

But this time, her emotions were too volatile—the Sphere was a life and death object—and she'd reacted before thinking clearly. Everything went crazy at once.

Her spells exploded into complete chaos. And she burned her house down.

She consoled herself with the fact that she hadn't lost all that much. She'd only been living there for a few months and hadn't yet brought all of her belongings from Salem. But, unfortunately, all of her magical tools were gone now. She was a lone witch without her tools, and with spells that needed those tools to succeed. And she had to do it surreptitiously, because she wasn't sure who—or how powerful her thieving enemy was. So, she set out to temporarily fix the problem as best as she could in her dire circumstances, borrowing the items she needed to cast the Locating Spell to find the Sphere.

She wouldn't allow herself to think of defeat. Or what she'd do after she retrieved the Sphere. If Evil was intent on gaining control of the Sphere, she'd need more than simple spells to guard it any more. She'd need more power, and help. Her family had been trying for years to get her to return to the coven but she's always felt like a freak there, unable to control something as important as emotions when spell casting. So, she remained a solo witch, guarding the Sphere, as was her destiny and her only goal in life. But now she was left wondering if being solo was the best idea.

Briana took a deep calming breath, exhaled softly, and then made one last thorough gaze around before making a dash to the back door of the shop. Assured that her emotions were under control—although the adrenaline was a heady tingle still present deep inside her—she muttered a quick spell to unlock the door. She grinned. The police were still trying to figure out how the thefts were being made when there was no sign of break-ins. A simple masking spell kept any cameras from catching her little forays too. Making sure she barely touched anything with her gloved hands, Briana closed the door behind her and moved into the dark interior of the small shop.

The copper salmon plaque hung on the wall above the spot where the copper pot had been displayed—before she'd borrowed it. She hurried over to the display window and slunk down in the shadows by the wall. She chomped down on a brief spurt of fear. This was crazy. Did she really need the salmon?

She already knew the answer to that. Her confidence was zilch since the disappearance of the Sphere. She couldn't trust her emotions—and thus her spells—and she needed all the help she could get right now. *Wisdom is a must. So stop stalling.*

Uttering a quick "Help me, Goddess," she reached up and grabbed the salmon plaque. As soon as she held it, she knew she was doing the right thing. She'd felt that same soul-deep assurance with each of the other items she'd borrowed.

Moments later she was dashing out the back door, relocking it, and then scurrying across the wide stretch of parking lot and back lawn into the surrounding shadows of the woods.

Exhilaration hit her like a punch to the gut. *Uh oh.* It was too late to stop the uncontrollable emotion. Her muttered "make my feet fly" spell instantly flip-flopped. And sent her spinning in the air like she'd been bowled over. She landed with a hard thud face down into a patch of poison ivy. Breath knocked out of her, she laid there for a long moment before she realized her predicament.

She scrambled to her feet already knowing the damage had been done. Not one for foul language she invented a few creative ones as she dejectedly walked away and headed back to Cynthia's house. "Great, just great," she said. "I needed this right now. So, not." Maybe if she got back to the house in time, she could whip up a potion and counteract the poison. She hurried her steps.

The huge old Victorian house where her elderly friend Cynthia lived sat on a cul-de-sac with two other homes. Three floors high, it looked proper and stately, and it accurately represented the wealth of its owner. The older woman was a widow, and a prominent citizen in Inverness. She was known for her generosity, her charities, and her odd eccentric projects. Briana had met her when she'd first moved there and had helped her with one of her charity projects. When her house had burned down, Cynthia had insisted that Briana move in with her until she could get another place. Since the older woman readily believed in the existence of witches, Briana didn't think it would cause any problems if any of her spells just happen to go crazy at any given time.

Of course, the one drawback was that Cynthia's youngest son was a cop and lived only blocks away. And he wasn't too happy with his mother's decision to let a stranger move in—especially one claiming the absurdity of being a witch of all things. He'd already promised to "keep an eye on you"— not so subtly warning Briana he suspected she was up to no good.

Since it was already after midnight, Briana was able to get back into the house without disturbing Cynthia. She hurried to her room with her newest acquisition, taking the stairs two at a time. Once she was in her bedroom she closed and locked the door before hiding the salmon plaque with the other acquired items in the back of her closet. Quickly stripping her clothes off she got in the shower and turned the nozzle on full force. The skin on her face and neck was already starting to itch and burn crazily and she had the bad feeling that she was too late. Poison ivy worked fast, darn it. She slopped on loads of lotion soap, scrubbing furiously.

The soap stung her skin, despite being made of oatmeal and chamomile. After she dried off she smothered a thick glob of chamomile cream on her face and neck. But nothing was helping to soothe the burning itch. Forcing herself to stay calm, she slipped on her favorite nightshirt, a silk T-shirt that reached just below her panty line and had the words *Sexy Witches Rule* in bold letters across the deep V-necked front. She shoved her feet into her bunny slippers, and then gathered her long hair in a loose knot on top of her head. She'd have to go down to the kitchen and whip up a magic potion to counteract the poison ivy otherwise she just might be in serious trouble by morning.

She was halfway down the stairs when she heard voices. She clearly heard Cynthia's voice and could tell the woman knew her visitors. Odd. She couldn't help thinking it was a really late time to be visiting. Shrugging her shoulders, she made a quick dash to the kitchen. Whoever Cynthia's late visitors were, she didn't need to be seen by them, wearing nothing but a skimpy T-shirt, bunny slippers, and her face and neck covered in thick face cream.

She gathered the necessary ingredients together and mixed them in a small bowl. Stirring the mixture gently, she left the kitchen and started back toward the stairs. Later she blamed it on her excruciating itchy skin distracting her and making her take a wrong turn. Muttering a healing spell under her breath and staring intently at the bowl she was holding while she thought of the particular words for the spell, she didn't realize she'd walked into the living room until she heard Cynthia choke out a small laugh.

Briana froze. *Oh my Goddess!* She looked up to find three pairs of eyes staring at her. Cynthia's, her cop son's, and another man's. Her mortified gaze locked instantaneously with the stranger's dark blue-grey eyes. She lost all sense of anything else in the room. Everything about him registered, undyingly embedding into her memory forever.

She could almost feel the magnetic pull of him reaching out to her, drawing her to him with starkly sensual threads like none she'd ever felt before. The incredible, heart-stopping realization shook her to the depths of her soul.

Her first coherent thought was that he had to be the sexiest, most captivating man she'd ever seen. Well over six foot-two-or-three, lean, subtly muscled, wide shouldered, slim hips, long legs, shoulder length midnight black hair, piercing dark blue-grey eyes, and a sculpted face that could grace the cover of a romance novel. *Whoa. Be still my heart.*

And that's when it happened. Arousal was her most dangerous emotion. In the blink of an eye, between one breath and the next, it hit her full force at the same time she mentally uttered the last words of the healing spell over the bowl she was holding.

The bowl flew from her hands and sailed unerringly across the short distance between them. Straight at the stranger! In one split second it struck, splattering the gooey mixture all over his face.

She was a witch in serious trouble. No doubt about it.

Chapter Three

Hunter froze in shock. He couldn't believe the woman had just thrown that bowl of goop in his face! Over his own muttered oath he heard his mother choke back a laugh, his brother guffaw loudly, and then the woman gasp, "Goddess, help me." Clenching his jaw, he slowly, meticulously wiped the mess out of his eyes and off his face. When he could see clearly again he shot his brother a murderous glare and muttered, "Shut up, Sloan."

Then he turned to the woman. He swallowed another curse word. Just moments ago he'd been standing there staring at her in lustful—make that *powerful* lustful—fascination as she walked into the room wearing that scandalous T-shirt over a sinfully perfect body made to torture any man's restraint. From head to toes she had a body models would kill for, curves in all the right places and soft smooth skin. His groin tightened instantly as he perused all that bare skin. She was petite but her legs were still long and slim, right down to her slender ankles. And her small feet were encased in large bunny slippers. He held back a sudden grin and brought his gaze slowly, thoroughly back up her mouth-watering figure. Her shiny, white-blonde hair was haphazardly piled on top of her head, and her face and neck were covered in a thick, white cream. All he could clearly see of her features were her startling, dark emerald green eyes. Then, just when he thought he was going to embarrass himself by drooling, she'd thrown that bowl of goop at him.

So much for lust. Hunter pushed away the erotic thoughts starting to creep into his head and pinned her with a hard stare. "Why the hell did you throw that at me? Are you crazy?"

The sexy siren slapped both of her hands on her cream-caked cheeks and squealed. "Oh! I'm so sorry! Honestly, I didn't mean for that to happen."

"Yeah right. The bowl just flew out of your hands by itself." Hunter gave her his best no-nonsense detective stare as he tried to keep from smiling at her adorable squeal. "Try the truth for a change."

"Now, Hunter," his mother cajoled gently, "Briana said she was sorry. Just because you're tired from your long flight doesn't mean you have to be rude."

Hunter shook his head, swallowing back a groan as his blood pooled low in his groin with a simmering heat. It wasn't exhaustion that had his body uncomfortably tight and tense. No, what he was feeling was far from it. And all because—despite her attack—the woman was his sole focus, every primal male cell in him reacting to her sensual allure. He let his gaze hungrily devour her one more time before he purposely clamped down on his lust and pushed it away again. Now wasn't the time or place. He didn't know anything about this strange woman—a woman his mother believed to be a witch of all things—and who was now living here. Sloan had already done a background check on her and came up with nothing.

Still, Hunter was inclined to agree with his brother that she was most likely a scammer out to get his mother's money. He bit back a snarl with the thought, hating that it might be true. It wouldn't be the first time that had happened. His mother was a too-trusting woman; a wealthy widow who believed everyone was honest and good.

Cynthia broke the uncomfortable silence. "Briana, honey, what do you have on your face?"

As if she was just realizing what she looked like—and what she was wearing—Briana uttered a small, embarrassed gasp and started backing out of the room. "I had an accident earlier and fell into a bed of poison ivy. I'll just go back to my room and—" She turned and ran.

Hunter breathed out a sigh of relief. Damn if that skimpy T-shirt and those ridiculous bunny slippers weren't keeping his libido on fire. He shook his head. Maybe he was beyond exhaustion if that was all it took to stir his lust. He was fast rethinking staying here. He wasn't entirely sure he'd be able to keep his lustful thoughts off the woman, especially since she'd be under the same roof. He and Sloan thought it a good idea to keep an eye on her for the brief time he'd be here, but now …

Sloan slapped him on the back and chuckled. "Must be something special about you, bro. She never threw anything at me."

"We startled her," Cynthia commented. "I learned early not to walk up on her suddenly."

Hunter searched his mother's calm features, his gut clenching in protectiveness. "What are you talking about, mom? Has she ever—harmed—you in any way?"

"No, dear, nothing like that." She patted his sticky cheek as she passed him and sat down on the sofa. "She's a witch, remember, and sometimes her little spells go awry. Startling her in the middle of one is sure to have a disastrous result."

Hunter sighed as he sat down in a chair opposite the sofa and finished wiping the goop off his face. "You've always been the most gullible woman I know when it comes to trusting people, mom. But honestly, she thinks she's a witch? She's either got a few screws loose—or she's a professional con."

"Hunter," Cynthia scolded gently. "I know it's your detective skills speaking that makes you automatically suspect her. But you have to trust me on this, son. She's a sweet, innocent woman down on her luck and as harmless as a child. Well, except when her spells backfire."

Sloan had filled him in on the background check but he wanted to hear more from his mother. He had the feeling that knowing as much as possible about Briana was a necessity he shouldn't ignore. "How did you meet her?"

Giving her son a sweet, calm smile, Cynthia indulged him and answered, "We met right after she came here. She was looking for a job and answered one of my ads for an assistant in the 'save the homeless pets' project. I immediately liked her. And don't frown, Hunter. You know I've never been wrong on my first impressions. So, anyway, after her house burned down she was homeless and I offered her a place to stay while she found a job and a new home."

"When did she reveal this witch idea she has?" Truth be told, that bothered him most of all. Why would such a beautiful woman indulge in such nonsense? Just his luck to be—unwillingly— attracted to a crazy woman.

"After we'd finished the project she mentioned that she was

looking for a job in a herbal shop or something similar. She wanted to work around stuff that was natural, you know, natural products, etc. But she wasn't having any luck finding a permanent job. Inverness isn't really that big of an area, you know. And she didn't want to have to drive to Tampa every day. Anyway, one day she was really upset when she came over to visit. I was having trouble with my prize roses—they were wilting in this heat wave—and she offered to 'spell' them to health. That's when she explained she was a solo white witch. Only, she has one major problem with her spells. If her emotions are involved when she spell casts, something goes wrong. She tried to heal my roses and instead ended up duplicating them. Honestly, you should have seen our faces when the entire garden, the front yard and the back yard, were suddenly overrun with roses. Everywhere."

Hunter's sharp detective mind raced through the possibilities of what could have happened. Witchcraft wasn't on his list of logical explanations. "It had to have been some kind of trick." He glanced at his brother. "Did you see anything, Sloan?"

Sloan shook his head. "Nope. I didn't visit mom until a few days later and she said that she and Briana cleared all the roses out before then."

"Get that look off your face right now, Hunter," Cynthia scolded. "At least have the decency to give me some credit. I'm not a gullible woman, and Briana is not tricking me in some crazy con. She hasn't asked for a dime. In fact, she's pretty much paid her own way the whole time she's been here. Her family sent her some money, and she's still diligently looking for a job. I swear," she continued in a frustrated tone Hunter didn't miss, "You two boys are so much like your father was. He doubted everyone's motives. You couldn't convince that man the sky was blue—even with the proof staring him in the face. I had hoped I raised you a bit better than that."

"Blame it on our career, mom," Sloan soothed. "And the fact that we love you so much that we tend to be over protective where you're concerned."

"Thanks, honey. But I'm warning you both right now. Leave Briana alone. Don't you dare scare her away."

Hunter let his brother soothe their mother, but he kept his thoughts to himself. His body may have reacted to her like any other red-blooded male would react to a sexy siren, but his gut was telling him to beware that particular siren's call. He had the feeling she wasn't all she let people see. He didn't for one minute think she was a witch—of all crazy things—but he did feel there was something different about her. And before he left here, he was going to find out what that difference was.

✳

The next day Sloan filled Hunter in on the details of the strange thefts around town. They did a drive by of each place hit: the novelty shop—which was now claiming another strike by the elusive burglar, the nursery where specific plants had been stolen, the herbal shop where only a few items had been taken—not necessarily expensive only odd, and then they went back to the novelty shop. There, the owner said the thief had stolen a copper plaque of a salmon. Hunter's thoughts were chaotic at the odd theft choices. He mentally went over the list of stolen items and couldn't make sense that any of the items were related in any way.

While Sloan took the report and checked the interior of the shop, Hunter searched out back of the shop for any clues. Since the store sat facing a busy street and was well lit on the front, he figured the thief had to have come in the back. As with the other strikes there was no sign of a break in. If it had only been this shop the thief had hit, twice now, his first thought would be that the perpetrator had a key. Especially since even the security cameras had been scrambled during the suspected time of entry. Hunter frowned. They were obviously dealing with a very good professional. But, why the hell would a thief that talented steal the particular items he had?

He meticulously studied the ground around the back of the shop and then slowly began to expand his search area. Yards away from the store he found a set of bushes. Easy place to hide while the thief made sure the area was clear before striking. He bent down near the closest bush and noted the ground was slightly indented as though someone had lay there for a few minutes.

He suddenly realized the seemingly dead foliage was actually a wilted poison ivy patch and quickly pulled his hand back from picking up a crumbled leaf.

Poison ivy. "Damn." Instantly his mind recalled the last words Briana had muttered as she'd fled the room last night. He abruptly stood, clenching his hands into fists as a bad feeling settled in his gut. He spit out an expletive. He really didn't want to put two and two together and come up with the logical answer that Briana had to have been here—last night. Hell, if he was right then his mother was housing a criminal. Okay, she was a beautiful sexy one—but still a criminal nonetheless. What the hell was going on?

Careful not to touch any of the potent leaves of the poison ivy, he knelt down and thoroughly searched the ground for any more clues. Minutes later he had to admit defeat. Who ever had been here hadn't left behind a trace of anything to go on.

So where did that leave him, other than with the gut feeling that Briana had been here? He returned to the shop with determined strides. No sense putting it off. A serious talk with the woman was in order before any more time passed.

Back at the house he found his mother working in her garden. "Hi, mom. Is Briana in the house?"

Cynthia shot him a suspicious look. "Why?"

Hunter gave her his 'mother can't resist' smile. "I just wanted to talk to her. I didn't get the chance last night." Reluctantly he mentally admitted that talking had been the last thing on his mind as he'd stared at the sexy siren the night before.

"If you're about to interrogate her, I won't let you. I'll just have to exercise a little tough love and tell you to go stay with your brother while you're here, Hunter."

He kept his smile plastered on his face. Damn, but the woman really had his mother under a spell. Maybe there was something to that witch idea after all. *Not.* "Warning taken, mom. I promise not to upset your little house guest. Now, where is she?"

"Downstairs in the basement. I let her use it for her spell work."

Hunter bit back a disgusted groan. He was already getting very tired of hearing about witchcraft. He stomped to the house and then down to the basement. As he approached the door he could hear soft chanting, lilting music, and smelled the distinct scent of sandal wood incense. Okay ... that caused him to stop in his tracks. The hairs on the back of his nape stood. A shiver of apprehension, the thought of facing the unknown, skittered over him.

He exhaled a harsh breath and took the last steps down into the open basement room. And stopped immediately.

Shocked.

Awed.

And ... suddenly, painfully aroused.

If he thought she was sexy last night wearing nothing but a skimpy T-shirt and bunny slippers, then he was wrong.

A naked Briana was far sexier.

Hell. She was breathtakingly sexy.

He was a doomed man.

Chapter Four

Briana looked up at the doorway just as she paused in her dancing around the room. Her breath whooshed from her. Hunter, a shocked expression on his handsome face, stood just a few feet away from her. Despite being suddenly breathless, she uttered a startled scream.

"Oh my Goddess!" Faster than she thought she could ever move she dove across the small space and grabbed her robe lying on the floor by the table. She never knew how she managed to get it on so fast, considering she was shaking so hard. Oh why, why hadn't she thought to lock the basement door? This couldn't turn out good no matter what she said or did now. She took a deep cleansing breath, deep into her lungs, and then slowly released it on a shaky sigh. Bracing herself, she lifted her head and reluctantly turned around to face Hunter.

The look in his piercing, hungry stare made her knees buckle.

She actually fell forward. Hunter took the few steps separating them in two long strides and caught her up against his hard body. In the split second it took her to wonder if witches really were capable of melting, she thought to clear her mind of any stray spells. A misfired spell right now wouldn't help this situation.

Stunned, she stared up into his handsome face and uttered a soft cry of shock as painfully arousing, electric waves arced between their bodies. This close she could see the intriguing dark grey flecks in the deep blue of his eyes. And she could see herself reflected back. It was disturbing—and yet exciting all at one time.

His arms felt like steel bands around her and there wasn't a spot on their bodies not meshed together. Lustful heat sank into her pores as it wafted off his hard body, and she went completely limp, feeling suddenly drunk on the primal sexuality he radiated.

His eyes darkened at her slight movement and he somehow managed to gather her closer against him. His firm, sensual lips parted on an intake of breath and he muttered, "What the hell is that?"

"That?"

"I feel like we're connected to a live wire," he answered hoarsely. One of his arms moved from her lower waist to slowly inch down her backside. She instinctively wiggled against the hard line of his erection pushing against her there. "Damn. Stop moving. I can't think straight."

Good to know she wasn't the only one feeling this incredible surge of lust. *But.* This was beyond crazy; she couldn't allow herself any kind of involvement—no matter how sexy the man happened to be—right now. She had one priority and she had to stay focused on that. *So not fair!*

"Maybe you should let me go," she suggested softly, and then berated herself for loving the fact that he actually hesitated by tightening his arms before he slowly released her.

"I should have listened to my gut instincts," Hunter muttered as he took several steps back. "I knew you were trouble the minute you threw that goop at me."

"Hey, that's not fair. I told you it was an accident."

"Right." He closed his eyes tight for a moment. When he looked at her again she nearly had a repeat of knees buckling; that look scorched her with a hungry heat she'd never felt before. "I'm not going to ask what you were doing down here. I'm not that crazy. Yet. Get dressed. Meet me upstairs." And then he turned and stomped out.

Briana stared with her mouth opened on an indignant "What?" Had he just ordered her to do his bidding? She glared, her usually very dormant anger surfacing. Who the heck did he think he was? Didn't he realize that she had enough power to turn him into something nasty like a toad—or worse—if he angered her to the point of no return?

No. He didn't realize it. She'd talked to Cynthia earlier that morning after Hunter had left with Sloan on a case. Cynthia had told her that Hunter didn't believe she was a witch. Normally that wouldn't bother her because she was used to such reactions and it

was a simple fact that people either believed you or they didn't.
But for some reason it did bother her this time. She tried to reason
it was because he was her dear friend's son. But she knew the truth
was she was attracted to him and that made her care about his
opinion. Darn. *Why now? Couldn't he have come into my life at a
better time?* Goddess, help her, if this was Fate's way of punishing
her for losing the Sphere …

✳

Hunter slammed down a large gulp of whiskey and welcomed
the burn in his throat and stomach. At least for the moment it kept
his mind off the burn in his groin. *Damn it.* He couldn't get the
picture of a naked Briana out of his mind. His erection strained
against his jeans and he grimaced with the pleasure-pressure. He
should have walked—no, ran—out of there. But then, he'd made
the mistake of touching her. *Double damn.* Until that moment he'd
never realized he had that much willpower in him. It had taken all
his reserves to keep from stripping that robe from her and taking
her to the floor. He'd never reacted to a woman that hungrily
before.

His first clear look at her features had stunned him. He knew
she had to be beautiful, her body had shown that. But when he'd
stared into those glittering emerald green eyes, he'd felt so lost he
couldn't even think straight. The rest of her features were incredibly
ethereal—she looked like some fairy princess out of a book. If he
were inclined to believe in witches, he'd almost swear she was using
a glamour spell. No woman could look that perfect, that sinfully
erotic and ethereal all in one.

Hell, he had to be reacting to her simply because she had a body
any man would fantasize about touching, and he had been celibate
for a long time now. Yeah, that was it. Simple lust. He could handle
it.

He turned to watch as she walked into the room, all thoughts
of being honorable flew right out of his mind. So much for heroic
vows. He cleared a throat gone dry. He could have sworn he told
her to get dressed …

"Do you always run around wearing a silk robe during the
day?"

A silk piece of cloth that clung to her like he had just minutes
earlier …

She smiled and it was like an invisible punch to his lower stomach. "Actually, I usually run around … like you found me in the basement." Her green eyes danced with sinful mischief. "Witches prefer to be naked most of the time. It helps—uh—center us."

Hunter growled under his breath. *Little minx.* "This 'I'm-a-witch' story isn't going to work on me, you know. I'm not gullible like my mother is."

She frowned at him. "That's very disrespectful of your mother, Hunter. Just because you don't believe in something as elemental as witches doesn't mean she's the not-so-smart-one."

"Ouch," he murmured, liking her spunk despite not wanting to. "Did you just call me stupid?" She blushed a lovely rose color and he had to bite back a groan of lust. Why something that innocent would streak a fireball through him was a mystery he didn't want to solve right then.

"Just stating a fact."

Speaking of facts … He'd almost forgot why he'd sought her out in the first place. Better for them both if he concentrated on what was important right now, and not how his body was on high lust-alert with her closeness. "Okay, sweetheart, we'll do the cliché 'agree to disagree' for the time being. Let's change the subject." He studied her face closely. Her skin was flawless, silky smooth and peach-toned. His hand suddenly itched to touch her and he clenched a fist. He mentally shook his head. *Concentrate, man.* "I see your little problem with the poison ivy wasn't serious."

He watched her intently for any telltale reaction. But then she turned away from him and walked over to stare out the window. Maybe that action was telling in itself. Might as well test her a little more. "Where were you last night that you accidentally ran into poison ivy?"

She shrugged her shoulders. "Did I say it was accidental? I misspoke. I was at a friend's house helping her clear out her back yard. Unfortunately she didn't warn me about the poison ivy there. Lucky for me—" she faced him with a grin that made him catch his breath at the sexy curl of her lips, "—my witchy skills saved me with that potion I made."

He wanted to believe her. That bothered him but it was better than the alternative. If she was lying, then there was every possibility she was the thief that had been striking everywhere around town.

Hell if he knew what he'd do if that turned out to be the case.

Wait a damn minute! "How the hell did you get it only on your face?" The rest of her body had to have been completely covered.

Briana sighed so dramatically he frowned even harder at her. "Didn't your mother tell me that you're a detective? It's simple, Hunter. I tripped and fell face forward into it."

"Without it touching you anywhere else on your body?"

With another teasing smile she quipped, "Duh. I was wearing gloves and—uh—I was fully clothed at the time."

Okay, he'd have to give her the benefit of the doubt. For now. Time to change tactics. He grinned purposely lustfully at her. Maybe catching her off guard would work better. "Fully clothed, huh? I'm sure that must be a rare sight." He let his hungry stare peruse her from head to toes and watched in fascination as her blush darkened, stirring the flames in his body up another notch. "Not that I'm complaining."

"You're a dangerous man, Hunter. I don't think I like you."

"You didn't say that with very much conviction, sweetheart."

"I save my convictions for my spells," she answered with both a tease and a warning in her tone. Catching the glint in her green eyes, he swallowed down another strong surge of lust. He liked her spunk. A lot.

He pondered her statement. Then, the words were out before he could stop them. "How about showing me one of your spells? That's if you really want me to believe you're a witch."

To his surprise her face paled. "I can't. Not at the moment."

"Why not?"

"Because, you non-believer, I have a little problem with my spells when I'm emotionally involved at the moment."

He just had to push. "Meaning?"

She growled at him! "Meaning that if you want to risk me turning you into a frog or something worse, then go ahead and tempt me, Hunter. Right now you've got me so flustered I can't even think straight."

"Flustered?" Now why the hell did that sound sexual? His whole body tightened, hot lust surging deep inside.

"Grrr. You are the most—the most—argh, just forget it! I'm out of here before I do something I'll regret."

"Come on, sweetheart," he tempted in a low voice. "Don't leave me dying of curiosity."

She searched his gaze for a long poignant moment. Hunter swallowed in sudden trepidation when her eyes narrowed and became green shards of fire. She slowly walked over to him and he forced himself to stand still.

"I wouldn't want to leave you dying with curiosity," she practically purred, "So, instead I'll leave you with what I'm feeling. Pure frustration. And there's no cure for it, Hunter. Not in this lifetime."

Before he could decipher what she was saying, exactly, she lifted up on her toes and kissed him. Shock and desire hit him so hard his whole body tensed painfully.

Her lips were soft. Incredibly soft and mouthwateringly sweet. And the kiss was all-too brief. He didn't have the chance to touch her or deepen the kiss before she was stepping back and then turning away. She glided out of the room so quietly he could have sworn her feet never actually touched the ground.

Hunter shook his head, body on fire, and thoughts so chaotic he didn't know what to do.

One thing was sure. Briana, aka siren, aka witch, was one potent combination of every man's fantasy woman. And he wasn't sure what he was going to do about her.

Chapter Five

Who would have thought a zoo could be so scary after dark? Briana forced her frozen feet to move again. She was sure her heart had stopped after that last scream. Darn peacock. Why the heck was he allowed to roam around free like that, giving him the perfect opportunity to sneak up on her and screech his head off?

And so much for her head-to-toes black burglar suit. She was so sure she blended into the shadows easily enough. She'd have to remember that peacocks obviously made good guard pets when needed.

"Okay, bird. Pull that stunt again and I'll turn you into a fried turkey." He was just lucky she hadn't been contemplating a spell when he'd frightened her like that.

She grimaced. Darn it. She hated having to be so careful with her powers. As long as she stayed calm, her spells were strong. But how often—lately—had she found herself actually calm? She'd been a bundle of nerves ever since the disappearance of the Sphere.

And having Hunter Dallas come into her life right now had been the proverbial straw-that-broke-the-camel's-back. Just being near him sent her into a whirlwind of emotions she had no chance of controlling. Any other time and she would have loved to explore this explosive chemistry building between them. But right now definitely wasn't the time. She had to focus on finding the Sphere.

She shuddered thinking of all the possibilities of what might have happened to the Sphere. An object of life and death, the Sphere had been sought over the centuries by both good and evil, wanting to control it. Eight inches high, in unbreakable glass, the oval sphere contained a miniature living willow tree. The willow represented "The Tree of Life." As long as the Sphere was in the protective care of the direct descendent of its creator, then the tree would continue to live.

And continue to keep the doors to the Underworld closed.

As long as that tree lived, the Underworld remained in captivity. Evil always found a way to escape, at one time or another, but the main doors that held back all Evil stayed closed.

Goddess, help them all if Evil had somehow managed to find a way to gain control of the Sphere. Killing the tree would open all the doors.

Panic threatened and Briana resolutely pushed it down. She had to stay focused. The last item on her list was a dove. Then she would have the necessary tools for the Divination Spell that would tell her where the Sphere was. She stood in the middle of the path that led to 'The Bird House' and glanced around for the peacock nuisance. The last thing she needed was another fright. Taking a calming breath in, she exhaled and centered her thoughts. Okay, time to get this over with.

A quick release spell opened the locked doors to the bird house and she slipped inside. With the exception of rustling here and there, a few quiet squawks, the huge aviary was relatively tranquil, all the birds settled in for the night. Knowing the doves would be naturally grouped together she started walking around the area carefully looking at each cluster of birds.

The dove represented a healing deity. She didn't need it as much for the locating spell as she actually needed it for the chance— the hope—that it would help control her emotions long enough to perform the spell safely. At this point she could use any little healing help available. She was so close to being out of control with her emotions and her spells right now, anything could happen. And that certainly wouldn't help the world.

The soft cooing led her to the dove nest in the far corner of the aviary. These particular doves were rare ones, found only in the deepest part of South America. Her instinct told her that no ordinary dove was going to work, so she'd sought out these.

"Hi, little ones," she murmured softly. Despite the little disagreement with the peacock earlier, she was an animal lover and had always been able to connect with them on a natural level. She had the unusual knack of being able to tame even the wildest animal with just a soft word and a gentle touch. "Which one of you will volunteer to come home with me for a short while? I promise to have you back as quickly as possible."

She slowly reached out her hand and gently petted the closest dove. It cooed encouragingly. She carefully lifted it from the nest and cuddled it close to her breasts. "As quick as possible, sweetie. You have my word on it."

Just as she started to turn away she heard the peacock outside scream again. But unlike his one-time screech at her, he was now continuing to wail over and over as though he'd turned into some kind of a warning siren. *Uh oh. That can't be good.* She had the bad feeling she was about to get caught. She couldn't take the dove now and still get out of here fast enough. She placed the little bird back in the nest and then hurried across the wide expanse of aviary back to the door. There, she stood in the shadows and cautiously peeked out to where the peacock was standing in the middle of the path screeching at the top of his lungs.

Just as she was beginning to think the darn bird had gone completely crazy, she saw the approaching figure of a man walking down the path. He walked as though he was cautiously taking each step, and he kept glancing around as though he expected someone to come out of the shadows. The hairs on her arms stood at attention, silently warning her of danger. Keeping tight control of her emotions she quietly muttered a quick revealing spell.

"Powers that Be, show me what I need to see. Make his true colors apparent only to me."

Her spell hit its mark, and despite the darkness of the night she saw his aura suddenly begin to glow all around him. It was dark red with dominant black. And it pulsed angrily. Definitely dangerous. She shivered in reaction. Who was he and what was he doing here? She bit back a moment of panic. And why was he heading straight to the bird house?

There was no way she could get out of here unseen before he got to the door, and no place for her to hide. She had no choice but to try a transportation spell.

And pray to the Goddess that she didn't end up in some place worse ...

Calm down. Stay calm. Calm. Center on calm. She repeated the mantra over and over as she watched the stranger come closer. But it was useless. She hadn't had control of her emotions since the disappearance of the Sphere. Panic was trying to rise and she was out of time. *One of these days I'm going to be able to control this.*

She took a deep, shaky breath and released it slowly. Then, just as the stranger was yards away from the door she quickly uttered the words to the transportation spell.

She didn't mean to have her last thought be of Hunter. Really, she didn't. But his face popped into her mind at the last moment, instantly bringing back the feel of his strong arms around her, and she murmured his name.

When she opened her eyes again she found herself lying on top of Hunter in his bed.

And this time, he was the one naked.

Startled. Angry.

And deliciously aroused.

Chapter Six

"That's an incredibly sexy outfit, darling," Hunter drawled in a low rumble as he wrapped his arms around her. His eyes were gleaming despite just being woken; lit with a simmering fire that took her breath away for one long poignant moment. "But I'm not sure how to get you out of it. Hidden zipper?"

Briana choked on a screech and tried to scramble free. "Oh my Goddess, this can't be real!" Could things have gone any more wrong? The last thing she had expected was to end up in Hunter's bed! Bed? She stopped her struggles immediately. Nope. It wasn't his bed she was on …

She lay fully stretched out on top of his hard, aroused body. And her struggling had somehow managed to align their bodies in just the right way; legs entangled, breasts to hard bare chest …

The feminine center of her that was already pulsing and begging for more of the hardness shoving up against it was aligned in just the perfect position. She groaned. He felt so good.

Hunter's answering groan startled her and her gaze locked with his. His blue-grey eyes stared hungrily back at her, and his breathing sloughed out roughly between his firm lips. She had the sudden urge to lean down and kiss him. The urge was so strong she had to bite her bottom lip for a distraction.

"I don't usually have a woman attack me in my sleep, sweetheart, but I'm not complaining." He grinned sexily. "Except, I'm a bit confused about the costume. Some kind of kinky preference?"

Briana's heart raced. She was wearing her cat burglar outfit! How the heck was she going to explain this? Her mind flew in different directions but she couldn't think straight lying there against all that male hardness and feeling his response pushing against her in the most intimate way. *Groan. Why don't I just embarrass myself and kiss him now while I wiggle harder against him?* His reaction couldn't be any more obvious. He thought she'd come into his room with the intent to seduce him. She couldn't let him find out what she'd really been doing.

"Sleepwalking," she blurted out in last moment desperation. "I didn't know what I was doing."

Hunter moved his hands up and down the length of her back and then to her butt. The pressing caress was slow and hot. "Hmm. Okay, that would explain the outfit." With an obvious firmer caress across one butt cheek, he frowned. "But I think I feel a bit insulted. Here I thought you were trying to seduce me."

"I wouldn't do that," she exclaimed, feeling her face heat with a telling blush. *Actually, it's a wonderfully yummy idea, but—not right now!*

"No? Pity."

Okay, that didn't have to sound so sexy! Then he moved slightly, arching up against her and she felt the delicious length of his hard erection press against her aching center in one hard push. *Oh my.* He was big. And so hot.

Time to get control of this before she ended up taking him up on his not-so-subtle offer! She pushed against his chest, eliciting another groan from him, and somehow managed to roll free of his arms to his side. She lay on her back and stared up at the ceiling trying to regain control of her emotions. Hunter exhaled a long harsh breath and then turned to prop on one elbow and stare down at her. She immediately closed her eyes against the fire she saw simmering in his. No sense in adding more fuel.

"Most sleepwalkers are wearing their night clothes when they leave their bed." His hot, thorough gaze roamed from the top of her head, slowly down her body, lingered on her gloved hands, and then stared at her feet encased in heelless leather boots. "For a woman who likes to run around naked, you're a bit overdressed right now." He frowned down at her and his sexy tone abruptly changed to wary. "What's the real truth, Briana?"

Darn. Darn. Darn! She was going to have to tell him some truth in order to keep his sharp detective mind from deducing the real reason she was dressed like this. "Okay," she said and then cleared her throat. "The truth is that I was performing a spell and it backfired. I didn't expect to end up in your bed, Hunter. Honest."

"How then did you end up on top of me?" He growled sexily. Her whole body responded and she almost turned back into his arms. Almost.

"It was a transportation spell." She frowned at his disbelieving snort then. So much for wanting him to hold her. "Deny it all you want, you non-believer, but that's exactly what happened."

"How stupid do you think I am?" Hunter lay back and stared at the ceiling. He muttered several expletives under his breath. "How much longer are you going to keep this charade going?"

Briana bit down on her bottom lip again. Obviously he wasn't going to believe her until she proved herself. And there was only one way to do that. She felt a moment of panic. Her emotions around Hunter were more than a little unstable. Using her magic to prove something right now wasn't her smartest idea.

But nonetheless, it was a matter of pride. She sat up and stared down into his stormy gaze. "Fine, Hunter. If you want proof then I'll give it to you. But you've got to promise me that you won't be angry if something goes wrong."

"Why would something go wrong? If you're a witch then you should be able to perform a simple spell, shouldn't you?"

The blush on her face heated up again at the sound of derision in his husky voice. "Well, um. Remember I explained that I have this little glitch in my skills. I can't guarantee my spells will work whenever my emotions are involved."

Holding her gaze with his, Hunter slowly sat up. "Explain about your emotions being involved."

Think fast, Briana. She couldn't let him know just how much he affected her. "Like right now," she quickly lied. "I'm upset about the transportation spell going awry. So, if I do another spell then chances are it would backfire even more crazily."

Hunter's features hardened. "I'm willing to risk it."

"Yeah. Right. Famous last words," she muttered under her breath.

"Come on, honey," Hunter coaxed way-too-sweetly. "Give it your best shot. I'm not scared."

You will be. She almost giggled at the thought. The comic relief was short lived. She made the mistake of letting her gaze move over him—and over his still very much aroused body part and she lost all coherent thoughts as her own body responded instantly. "Um. Would you mind covering up? I don't need the—uh—distraction."

His slow grin was so sexy, so hot it caused her to nearly melt on the spot. Still holding her gaze captive he slowly reached over and pulled the coverlet over the bottom half of his body. The blanket tented and he grinned wolfishly. She choked back a gasp of pure lust. Darn but the man was too sexy for his own good. *And he knows it, too!*

She hastily cleared her wayward thoughts and went to work to calm her emotions. It wasn't easy. He was too close. Too hot. Too male. *Calm. Center your calm.* She mentally repeated the mantra over and over for several long minutes. And all the while his heated stare never left her face.

Finally, she hoped she was ready. She glanced around the room. It must have been his room when he was still living at home. Decorated in masculine colors, with sports memorabilia scattered everywhere. On a dresser across the room were several family photos. In one was a picture of Hunter as a young boy standing beside a pony. *Perfect. That will work.*

She meant only to levitate the photo across the room to Hunter. Of course, it didn't work out that way.

"Across the space, come to me.
Bring back the past, for Hunter to see."

Poof! She groaned loud, completely disgusted. *Oh no, there wasn't supposed to be a poof!* When the white mist cleared, she cringed and covered her face with her hands choking out another frustrated groan.

Hunter spit out so many stark, rough expletives she was shocked at the tirade. But she couldn't blame him. She wanted to say a few choice words too.

Standing at the foot of the bed was the—very much alive—pony from the picture.

"It could have been worse," she whispered in an embarrassed tone. "I could have turned you into the pony."

"No way in hell am I'm seeing this," Hunter muttered, his voice sounding shocked and angry at the same time. "It has to be some kind of illusion trick."

The pony took affront to that and neighed. Loudly. Hunter slowly pulled his shocked gaze from the pony to finally stare at her. "You're good, baby," he bit out hoarsely. "I'll give you that. But I know this is a trick. And you're not leaving this room until you explain in full detail how you did this."

Briana opened her mouth to blast him with an angry response but then shut it. His detective mind wasn't going to accept the reality of witchcraft, no matter what she did. His whole concept of life in general was ordered and concise, a logical explanation for everything that happened. His rejection bothered her, but she couldn't do anything about it for now.

She waved her hand at the pony. "Return to the past. Let memories forever last." With a *poof* the pony disappeared in a cloud of smoky mist. *At least that worked right. If only everything else was that easy.* She got off the bed. Hunter muttered the order "Stay," in a deadly quiet tone and she shivered in response. But she shook her head at him.

"Sorry. I did my best. I can't force you to believe, Hunter."

"A simple explanation," Hunter grit out, "would suffice for now. Did you use some kind of illusionary powder? Something that made me think I was seeing what you wanted me to see?"

Briana sighed, suddenly feeling very tired. It had been a long night. And Hunter's disbelief was wearing on her emotions harder than anything else ever had. She turned and walked to the door. "Goodnight, Hunter."

Despite the threat he muttered at her as she opened the door, she still forced herself to walk out. Never in all her life had she wanted someone to believe in her like she wanted him to do now. It wasn't so much that she needed him to believe in her witchcraft.

It was that she needed—wanted—him to simply believe in her.

How mixed-up crazy was that?

Chapter Seven

At least this time when she entered the room she was almost fully dressed, Hunter thought with a wry grin. His body tightened in instant painful arousal. That's if you could call that damn outfit fully dressed. His hungry gaze watched her cross the breakfast room to the buffet bar. A flimsy, lacy blouse looking more like a sexy negligee top dipped low at her breasts, and sat daringly high above her navel, clinging to her like a silk glove, and showing an enticingly amount of soft bare skin. Sleeveless with thin straps, there wasn't much to it besides the dainty lace. Damn, it was beyond sexy. It was temptation and danger, all in one, to any red-blooded male. He groaned, allowing his gaze to go lower. Her low, hip-hugging jeans looked like she'd been poured into them. For a long, arousing moment he contemplated about how hard it would be to get her out of them. His gaze slowly, hungrily caressed over her hips, butt, and long legs. His mouth watered with the erotic thoughts bombarding him and he bit back another lusty groan.

Then he choked on the mouthful of food he'd just tried to swallow as his gaze dropped to her feet. Bunny slippers. Damn, why should that be so sexy? He couldn't help it. He chuckled.

Briana turned to look at him with one slender brow rising in question. "Ah," she noted, "You're a morning person. What's so amusing?"

"Nothing," Hunter answered, reluctantly forcing the erotic thoughts out of his head. No way in hell was he going to tell her that she kept him hard as nails—dressed or not. "I was just wondering if you're one of those people that have cold feet all the time."

She blushed prettily as she sat down at the breakfast table. "You've figured me out. These slippers are my most comfortable pair of shoes." Breaking her gaze from his, she quickly changed the subject. "Where's your mom this morning? She's usually here when I come down for breakfast."

"She had an early appointment at the Community Center with the director there. Her latest pet project is keeping her busy." He sat back in his chair and studied her closely as she tried to act like she was ignoring him and began to eat. Damn, but everything she did was sexy. Her movements were delicate, graceful, and he suddenly realized he could watch her for hours and never get bored.

Careful. That range of thoughts didn't bode well. He was a confirmed bachelor, the love-them-and-leave-them type of man. Getting involved right now when his life was so unstable wasn't the smartest idea. Especially with this particular woman. He still wasn't sure about her. And after last night's event, he was even more cautious. How the hell had she pulled that illusionary stunt? Just the thought that she could so easily pull a trick like that on him, and he not be able to find a feasible explanation, was grating on his nerves.

"We need to talk about last night," he stated. She immediately stopped eating and slowly lowered her fork to her plate. Then she raised her head and pinned him with a hard emerald glare. Man, he was betting she had a temper that could scorch the hide off a man if he wasn't careful.

"There's nothing more to talk about," she answered, her voice firm. "You wanted proof and I gave it to you. It's your choice if you believe what you saw or not. What more do you want from me, Hunter?"

Now there was a loaded question! He shifted in his chair, his jeans uncomfortably tight with the obvious answer that popped in his head. He cleared his throat. "Okay, sweetheart, point taken. I choose to not believe. I think there's a logical explanation for what you did, and I'll figure it out sooner or later. Now," He smiled slowly, unable to keep the obvious hunger from his tone, "Let's talk about you coming to my room dressed in that sexy body suit."

"I explained that."

"Yeah, right. You were doing a 'transportation spell' and it backfired. Tell me, sweetheart, do you always dress like that while performing that particular spell? What happened to the 'no-clothes-necessary-while-playing-witch' explanation?"

She blinked innocently at him, sending his heart rate up. She looked nothing short of adorable as she smiled sweetly at him. It made him all the more wary of her. "You can't get past that naked idea can you, Hunter?"

Damn little minx. He grinned back at her. "I have to admit it stays in my mind more than it should where you're concerned."

✳

Uh oh. Briana felt her cheeks heat again at his words. He could drawl them out with the sexiest tone she'd ever heard a man use. Not good. Hunter was a dangerous man, in more ways than one, to her right now. She couldn't let him get close. And no matter what … she couldn't fall for him. She almost groaned aloud. She had the bad feeling that fighting the urge to fall for him was going to be a losing battle. *Goddess, help me.*

She had planned on performing the spell tonight, at midnight. It was the 'Witching Hour' and should help her incantation be all the stronger. But now she wasn't so sure about the timing. She hadn't slept last night after retreating to her own room. Try as hard as she could she couldn't get past the thought of lying on top of Hunter's hard, aroused body for all too brief a time. She hadn't had control of her own aroused emotions ever since. If she chanced the spell tonight—feeling this overly attuned with Hunter—Goddess knew what disaster would occur.

But time was running out. The Sphere had to be in her possession or the Tree would start to wither and eventually die. That couldn't happen! Suddenly nervous and uncharacteristically agitated she pushed back from the table to stand. Her hand accidentally knocked over her coffee cup. The steaming hot liquid splashed across the exposed skin of her lower belly and she gasped out with the pain.

Hunter jumped to his feet and came around the table. He grabbed her cloth napkin and quickly pressed it against the wet burn. "Damn, honey, that's going to leave a bad spot. Hold on and I'll get a cool cloth."

Briana took in a deep inhale of his male scent, immediately recognizing his arousal mixed with his concern. It was a heady combination. She stopped short of swaying into him. "I'm fine," she murmured.

"Far from it," Hunter muttered. "But that's a different topic of conversation better left for later. Right now, we need to get something on that burn. It's already starting to blister."

Without consciously thinking about it, she immediately uttered a small healing spell. *Oh no!* She couldn't stop the words in time. Would she ever learn?

Hunter had a split second to react. After one shocked expletive, he grabbed her and shoved her to the floor, his body instinctively, protectively covering hers. At the same time, all the dishes in the room started sailing around in total chaos and all the silverware became instant missiles of deadly accuracy. He cussed a blue streak as some of the utensils and dishes hit against his back but he kept her covered completely.

Briana cringed at each stark expletive he spit out, knowing he had to be hurting with every missile strike. She moved her head slightly and whispered against his neck, "I'm so sorry."

Hunter suddenly stiffened. He raised his head and stared down at her, still keeping her face protected with his hands. He stared hard at her, looking deep into her eyes. The blue-grey depths of his gaze swirled with some unexplained emotion she couldn't quite decipher. Then he took her by complete surprise by huskily drawling, "Kissing you right now would only make the situation more volatile wouldn't it—if you tried to calm all this down?"

Huh? She was stunned. Was he saying what she thought he was? That he believed her now? And she didn't dare dwell on that kissing part ...

So she shook her head. "I need to be calm."

Amidst the splattering of plates hitting floor and walls, another barrage of utensil missiles landed all around them, some hitting Hunter's back again. He cussed. Desperate she pleaded, "Help me, Hunter. I need calm."

He suddenly grinned at her. "How about those Cubs? Think they'll win the Divisional this time?"

Great. Just that quick, with his too-sexy smile, she was back to thinking about that kissing part again. Because she really wanted to kiss this man senseless. He was so incredible! Instead she grinned and then uttered the ceasing spell, hoping against hope that it would work. Immediate calm reigned. All the airborne dishes and utensils dropped to the floor.

Hunter didn't move. He stared down into her eyes, mesmerizing her with the intent look shining in the dark blue depths. Every spot their bodies touched, heat ignited. His hard erection pressed against the juncture of her jeans and she wanted to wiggle against him just to feel him push deeper, harder against her. Instead she bit her lip and remained still.

She took a deep breath and then slowly released it. "You believe me now?"

Hunter slowly shook his head. "I don't know what to believe." He seemed to think about it for a long moment. "It's possible you have some kind of telekinetic talents. The fact that your emotions are involved would tie in with the way objects fly every time you lose control. I've heard of that phenomenon."

Briana sighed. He still didn't believe her. And why the heck should that hurt so much? She sighed. "You're right. That must be the explanation."

Hunter frowned at her dejected tone. Before he could say anything they heard a loud crash from somewhere in the house. Briana looked confused.

"I didn't do anything else," she muttered defensively, "Honest."

Hunter surged to his feet then reached down and pulled her up beside him. "I know, honey," he assured her. Briana suddenly shivered at the serious tone in his voice. "That sound came from the back door. Since mom was scheduled to be gone all morning, I'm assuming it's not her breaking into her own house. Stay here while I check it out."

"Someone brave enough to burglarize in broad daylight?" Briana followed him to the hall. "That's crazy."

"Yeah?" Hunter grimaced. "Since being around you I'm starting to realize that crazy is the normal state of being, around here." He put a restraining hand at her waist and pushed her back. "Damn it, Briana. Stay right here."

She frowned at him but stopped. He was a detective after all. He could handle a simple burglary. The hair on her nape suddenly rose, and a shiver of apprehension skittered across her skin. Her instincts were suddenly telling her this wasn't a simple break in. A picture of the strange man at the zoo last night popped into her mind. There had been something—weird—about him. His aura had pulsed with danger and evil. Had he followed her? Who was he? What was he after?

Before she could move or call out to Hunter she heard him grunt out a few nasty expletives. Heart in her throat she hurried to the back entrance of the house. She skidded to a halt when she found him sitting on the floor by the open door, rubbing his head, and cussing words she wasn't sure really had any meaning at all. She hurried over and knelt beside him.

"What happened?"

"Damn intruder hit me from behind. He was already inside."

Briana quickly perused the area. The door was wide open. There was no sign of anyone else, but the strange feeling of danger in the air still lingered. "What did he hit you with?"

"Damned if I know. It felt like a brick." He examined his hands. "But there's no skin broke, no blood. What the hell could hit me that hard and knock me down and yet not leave a mark?"

She had an idea, but she didn't dare voice it. He probably wouldn't believe her anyway. She'd suspected last night that the stranger had some kind of powers. The subtle hint of dark magic had been interwoven in his red and black aura. What he was doing here and why was now a mystery that had suddenly become priority to solve. She had the bad feeling it might have something to do with the missing Sphere. *I'm running out of time.*

Hunter stood and pulled her up with him. He searched her face, noting her concerned expression, and then touched her cheek with a gentle caress. "It's okay, honey. He's gone." He waved a hand in the direction of the back yard. "Not a trace of him; he's probably still running." He looked closer at her, touching her arm. "Why are you still trembling?"

She wanted to tell him, came close to letting the words spill from her mouth, but instead she chewed on her bottom lip and then lied. "I just can't get over the fact he was brave enough to burglarize in the day time."

Hunter frowned. "I'd say it was because he's most likely an amateur, but with the odd thefts happening around town lately, I'm not so sure now. My main concern is why he chose Mom's house."

She knew why, and the truth made her tremble all the harder. Hunter noticed immediately. With a soft, "Poor baby," he pulled her into his arms. She settled against his hard chest in the pretense that she was scared about the intruder, and let him comfort her. Her mind raced with the possibilities of who the stranger was and why he was here, and most importantly what exactly she was going to do about it.

Hunter cuddled her close, the heat from his body wafting subtly into hers. He moved one hand up her back to her shoulders, and his other hand slid down to her lower back. She felt him stiffen, his whole body hardening against hers.

All thoughts of danger and the intruder went right out of her mind. Even knowing she shouldn't, she couldn't stop herself. She pressed closer to him, aligning her body in just the right way so that his hard erection was nudging insistently, right where she needed it to be. Hunter groaned and pushed against her.

"Damn, but you are a contradiction I can't figure out," he muttered against her bent head. "One minute you're all sweet and vulnerable. Then the next moment, you're every man's fantasy come to life." He tangled his hand in her long hair and tugged her face up from his chest. "Do you do it deliberately?"

She managed to keep her expression as innocent as possible. "Do what?"

His dark eyes glittered with hunger, but his expression clearly showed her he wasn't happy with the way he was reacting to her.

"Come on, sweetheart," he drawled. "You're not as innocent as you want everyone to believe. You know what I'm talking about."

"I don't profess to be innocent," she replied, trying to keep the sudden hurt from being so obvious in her voice. "You're the one who pulled me into your arms. Don't blame me for any reactions."

Hunter tightened his fisted hold on the handful of hair and tugged her face closer to his. Briana held her breath. She'd never seen such stark hunger in a man's expression before. It sent her nerves tingling, her body threatening to overheat, and her heart to racing. His words came out rough and low, "Why do I have this bad feeling that keeping you at arm's length will turn out to be as—dangerous—as keeping you in my arms?"

Dangerous? Why the heck would he say something like that? She frowned at him. "Honestly, Hunter. You can be the most dramatic man. Why don't you just admit that you want to kiss me and get it over with?" *Oh! Why did I say that?* She stopped short of shaking her head at the mental denial. This was all his fault. He was the one who had brought the kissing subject up earlier and now she couldn't get it out of her mind.

Hunter's sexy mouth curved into a slow, sensual smile that stole her breath. He tightened his arm around her lower back and pulled her closer. Then, his hand lowered and caressed over her backside before tightening on her bottom. His long fingers curved around the globe, teasingly resting in the crevice between. One hard shove against her had his erection pressed so tight and snug between the vee of her legs that it felt like they had both somehow become naked. She gasped with the incredible, intense feeling.

Hunter caught the sound with his mouth. His hard, hot lips claimed hers in an open mouth kiss so erotic it sent her senses crazily reeling in a split second. She lost all coherent thoughts. She was melting. She wrapped both her arms around his neck and clung to him as he kissed her senseless. And Goddess help her, but the man could kiss like no other man.

Hunter released his grip on her hair and moved his hand down to her neck. Her heart was beating so hard and fast she was sure he felt the racing pulse under his hand as he caressed there and then moved lower. They were pressed so tight against each other she wasn't sure how he managed to wedge his hand between them and curl it around one of her breast. But he did, and she uttered a small squeal of pleasure into his devouring mouth. He responded by squeezing lightly, and moaned a starkly hungry sound that seemed to reverberate up from his chest straight into hers.

She couldn't breathe. He was slowly devouring her with an erotic intensity that had her panicking and yet mentally begging for more. She had to think. There was a reason this couldn't be happening. What was it, again?

Just when she knew she had to stop this before things got completely out of control, Hunter suddenly broke the kiss. She gasped in much needed air and stared, stunned.

Breathing hard, he huskily murmured, "Anything flying around?"

Okay, she knew that had to mean something but couldn't wrap her chaotic thoughts around it. "What?"

He leaned his forehead against hers, briefly touching her lips again with another hard, quick kiss. "Nothing," he muttered. He stared intently at her mouth, his lips hovering, his breath hotly wafting over hers. "God, Briana, you have the sweetest, softest mouth I've ever tasted. I want to taste it again." He closed his eyes for a moment, his sensual features hard and flushed. "But my gut instinct is telling me to release you before this gets out of control." He groaned, hard. "And I've never ignored my instincts."

To her dismay he suddenly released her and stepped back. She almost fell forward into his arms again—wanting to be there more than wanting her next breath. That realization shocked her deeply.

Before either of them could say anything more, Sloan walked in through the open back door. He stared at them, instantly noticing Briana's flushed features and Hunter's hard frown.

"Did I—uh—interrupt anything?"

"What are you doing here, Sloan?" Hunter's voice was rough, and Briana noticed he was still standing like a stiff statue after releasing her.

"Whoa, bro. Sorry." He glanced at her, raising his brow, but Briana just shook her head. She knew this brother trusted her no less than Hunter did, and she couldn't help but be hurt by the fact that neither one had ever given her a chance. Sloan looked back at Hunter. "I thought I'd take you to lunch and discuss our 'odd' case. Something new has come up."

Hunter ran a hand over his face. "Yeah, sounds good." He slanted a glance at Briana but never let his eyes meet hers. "Lock the doors behind us, and set the alarm. Mom must have forgotten to do that this morning." He seemed to hesitate for a moment, and then with a muttered expletive under his breath he walked out the door with Sloan right behind him.

Briana sighed out shakily. And he'd called her a contradiction! One minute he was kissing her senseless, and the next he was acting like it had never happened.

She moaned, and then muttered aloud, "Whatever I do, I will not utter any spell words right now. I will remain calm." With the way she was feeling right then, she just might end up inadvertently destroying the world! Yep. This was definitely all Hunter's fault.

She shook her head. Who was she kidding? She had to admit it, whether she wanted to or not. Given the chance again, she'd willingly fall right back into his arms.

And she knew, soul deep, that she'd do anything it took to stay there.

Chapter Eight

When she finally managed to gain complete control of her emotions, Briana made a sweep of the back yard looking for any clues to the intruder. Just as she'd suspected, he'd left no physical traces. She had no choice but to try a spell to look for any magical trail.

Checking to make sure no one was around to witness her magic, she stood in the doorway of the back door and softly chanted the words for a clarity spell. "Bright as day will be his path. Show me the source of his power. Bring forth his motive and need. This I command, so mote it be."

Even though she was as calm as possible, there was still a long moment when she panicked thinking her magic was about to go crazy. The air around her suddenly appeared like a visible heat wave rolling across the back yard. She braced herself for the collision as it rapidly flowed straight at her.

Just as she started to close her eyes against the wave, everything around her seemed to distort and blend into blurry shapes. She blinked in confusion. *What's going on?* What was she seeing? She rubbed her hands over her eyes and then looked again.

The entire backyard had turned into a scene straight out of a history book.

Instead of a wide expanse of green lawn, a dark emerald green glen appeared. "A glen?" She felt an odd, sudden sense of familiarity. Her ancestors were from the once-mystical country of ancient Scotland and she'd grown up hearing stories about the incredibly beautiful glens there. Every one of her relatives knew his or her Scottish history from centuries back. Some deep, inner instinct told her she was now looking at a place that had to have been—or still was—a familiar spot for any of the guardian witches.

But there was something else odd about the illusion. The glen looked wild and untamed. She had the undeniable, strong and distinct impression that she was looking at a place that had yet to know human—or witch—intrusion.

"Why show me this?" she voiced aloud. What did the mysterious glen have to do with the intruder? How could one so obviously evil have anything to do with such a hallow place of serenity and beauty?

She was still trying to figure out the connection when the visible heat-wave air suddenly shimmered. In the blink of an eye, the backyard was returned to its original state. "Darn. What the heck am I supposed to do with that information?" And she still didn't know anything more about the mysterious stranger. This was getting her nowhere fast, and time was running out. The Tree of Life wouldn't last much longer out of her possession. She forced back the threatening panic. Then made up her mind. She was going to do the Location Spell tonight. She didn't have a choice. It was definitely a matter of now or never. She could feel it with every instinct in her.

And in order to perform the spell with complete concentration and no emotions involved, she had only one major thing she would need to do.

Not think about a too-sexy-for-his-own-good Hunter.

✳

It was definitely easier said than done. "Good intentions never work out," she mumbled as she pushed her hair out of her eyes and looked up from her spot on the ground at Hunter's feet. He towered over her, arms crossed over his wide chest, and an all-male grin tugging at his sensual lips that had her heart racing out of control.

It was late evening and she had managed to avoid him all day. He and Sloan had come home for lunch with their mother and she'd purposely left the house to do errands. When they were present for dinner she had determinedly gone out for a fast-food pick-up.

Who would have thought the man would have discovered her in the back yard trying to climb a tree. Granted, she had a good excuse. She wanted the bird eggs she'd seen earlier. Every little ingredient for her Spell was that much more help in assuring she succeeded. And climbing a tree to get those eggs seemed like an easy task. At first.

"At least you didn't try climbing ... naked," Hunter drawled in a low sexy tone. "That would have certainly hurt." He slowly shook his head, and then chuckled when she discreetly rubbed at her sore bottom. "Hard landing, sweetheart?"

"It's all your fault," she told him with a glare. "You startled me. I was almost to the ground when you snuck up on me. Why the heck are you out here sneaking around anyway? Don't you have better things to do?"

"You tell me why you were out here climbing a tree in the dark and then I'll tell you my reason." He gave her a long searching look that covered her from top to bottom. Before his gaze met hers again she felt decidedly scorched. "Damn, baby. Your contradictions drive me crazy. You're either running around deliciously naked or you're wearing clothes so tight I can't help but wonder if you were poured into them. Didn't those damn tight jeans split when you fell?"

Actually, they had. But she wasn't going to admit it! "Go away, Hunter. You don't really want to know why I was climbing the tree, and I don't want to verbally spar with you anymore."

Hunter reached out a hand. "Nope. I'm not in any hurry to leave. Need a hand up?"

Grrrr. The aggravating man! "Why are you out here stalking me?"

His expression sobered. "We need to talk, Briana. You've been avoiding me all day, and I'm getting tired of waiting."

"Talk about what?"

"We'll talk back in the house. Now, give me your hand, sweetheart."

"Go. Away." If he kept torturing her like this, always making her think about him, she wasn't going to be able to do what she desperately needed to do tonight. Her feelings for this man were already past controlling and she couldn't deal with that right now. Saving the world was more important.

Hunter muttered something under his breath and suddenly leaned down. He grasped her by the waist and hauled her up, straight into his arms. She gasped in surprise. And then in pain.

"Ouch. I think I may have twisted my ankle when I fell."

Hunter didn't hesitate. He swung her up into his arms. He

turned back to the house and started walking. "At least you can't run from me now."

"I'm beginning to think you're a bully, Hunter Dallas."

"And if I believed in witches, I'd swear you are one, Briana Adair," he countered smoothly. "You're too ... mysterious ... for a man's peace of mind."

"What's that supposed to mean?" And he accused her of being contradictory!

"Only that you're not getting out of my sight tonight until I have some answers."

Being held in his arms like this was doing crazy things to her heart ... and her body. She couldn't even think straight. And she desperately needed to. "Answers to the mystery of life?" Desperation making her tone angry she glared and rushed on, "Of witches? Okay, Hunter. Here're your answers. Yes, Virginia, there really are witches. And yes, they do have magical powers. Want me to turn you into a toad or something?"

"Keep up the sarcasm, baby, and I'll have to resort to something drastic to shut you up." His wicked grin started invisible butterflies spinning in her stomach. "Instead, let's play a game. I'm the big, bad detective. And you're the suspect."

Did Hunter suspect her in the burglaries? How? She'd been so careful. Sloan hadn't even discovered any clues. She cleared a throat gone dry. "I'd rather talk about that drastic measure you mentioned. What will you do, tape my mouth shut? Are you brave enough to take that chance? Maybe I can spell cast with my eyes as well as my mouth. Maybe all I have to do is think about you being turned into a toad, and poof, you're a toad. So don't threaten ... Oomph!"

Her last words were swallowed by Hunter's mouth. She had the brief moment to be thankful he was holding her in his arms because otherwise she'd have fallen right then. She had already experienced that his kisses were intoxicating and could render her senseless in mere seconds, but shouldn't someone have warned her that a second round would threaten her heart's shaky determination to keep him at arm's length and make her forget why getting involved right now was not the thing to do?

Reluctantly, she managed to turn her head and break free of his hard kiss. "That is so not fair, Hunter." She bit back a groan at the husky tone of her voice.

Hunter stared down at her as she slowly laid her head on his shoulder. His dark blue eyes shone with an obvious hunger that made her breath stall, and she had to remember to breathe again. His own breathing was harsh but he quickly got control and sighed out a rough exhale. "I've had to use a lot of different—drastic— measures to control a suspect, baby. But kissing someone quiet is a definite first." He groaned. "Do me a favor and don't make me have to do it again. I'm not sure kissing you is the smartest thing I've ever done."

She frowned at him. "I think you just insulted me." She was glad her voice sounded obviously indignant but the truth was she was scared. That was twice now in just a few minutes that he'd referred to her as a suspect. This definitely didn't bode well. "You could have just told me to stop talking. If kissing me was such a 'job' to you, then don't worry about having to do it again. I'll make sure of that."

He remained silent. Slanting a quick glance at his face she tried to decipher if he was angry. Or was it something else that had his sensuous lips set in a hard slash and his handsome features a bit flushed under his tan?

Hunter carried her into the house and then into the living room where Sloan was waiting. "That's where the 'suspect' part comes into play, sweetheart," he finally responded. "I can't trust your word." He placed her on the sofa and then stared down at her. She barely heard his muttered words, "I wish the hell I could."

Their gazes remained locked for a long poignant minute. Sloan cleared his throat, breaking the subtle, sensual spell cocooning them.

"Let's get this over with, Hunter, before Mom discovers what we're doing."

She looked from Hunter to Sloan and then back again. Despite their 'I'm-a-detective-and-I-take-no-prisoners" expressions, both men looked a bit uncomfortable. What was going on? She chewed on her bottom lip, worrying it between her teeth. Whatever was going on was sure to spell disaster for her. She could feel it with a deep certainty that left her shivering.

She finally managed to speak past her trepidation. "Why do I have this feeling I should start screaming for Cynthia to come save me?"

"Open your mouth to try," Sloan threatened, coming to stand next to Hunter. "And I'll have it taped shut so fast you won't get the chance to squeak out the first word."

"Sloan," Hunter growled under his breath. "Drop the 'mean cop' attitude."

Briana took a deep breath and then released it on a shaky exhale. "What's going on? Am I being interrogated?"

"We just have a few questions, Briana," Hunter said, a hard edge to his tone. "And this would go a lot easier on you if you would be honest in answering."

Okaayy. Might as well get this over with. She could clearly hear a mental clock ticking, warning her time was running out. "Ask away."

Hunter looked away for a moment and then abruptly asked, "What—type of tools—does a professed witch need?"

She narrowed her eyes at him. "Professed?"

His sensuous lips hardened into a thin line of anger. "Just answer me."

She shrugged, stalling for time, afraid of what was coming next. "It would depend on what the real witch needed certain tools for. Why?"

Sloan handed her a piece of paper. "If you were a witch needing certain tools, would this list be a priority?"

She read the list. Antique copper pot. Copper salmon plaque. Incense. Smudge stick. Candles. Plants. *Uh oh.* She was a witch in deep trouble. How had they figured it out? She'd been so careful. She was dismayed to see her hand shaking as she handed the list back to Sloan.

Avoiding Hunter's intense stare, she nodded her head. "Yes. This list indicates a good idea of what might be needed or used." There was no sense in lying at this point. They weren't dumb, and she didn't want to make the situation any worse than it already was.

"Hell, Briana," Hunter ground out between clenched teeth. A muscle jumped in his clenched jaw. "What are you up to?"

She desperately wanted to say anything but the real truth. Saying it aloud would make it too … real. But, with her gaze caught in Hunter's stormy one, she suddenly realized that she couldn't do it anymore. She didn't have the time to spare.

"Fine." She straightened her shoulders, centered her calm, and stated, "I know you're not going to believe this but I'm going to tell you the truth. I needed those items for a special—a very important—spell. If I don't complete the spell, then something horrible will happen."

"Horrible?" Hunter spit the word out in obvious disgust. "Being overly dramatic, aren't you?"

She opened her mouth to reply. The lights went out. Her heart stuttered then instantly began racing in total dread and fear. "Yes, Hunter. Horrible. And something tells me it's already starting."

"Must be a blown fuse," Sloan stated. He could be heard rummaging around in a drawer. He flipped on a flashlight. Briana blinked in the glare of the flash as he pointed it directly at her face.

"Check outside," she said, trying desperately to keep her growing fear at bay until she could logically figure out what to do next. "You're going to see the entire city is blacked out."

"Bloody hell," Sloan exclaimed. "She's right, Hunter. There's not a light anywhere."

Hunter reached down and clasped Briana's arm and then pulled her up next to him. "Start explaining, Briana. What the hell do you think is going on?"

For one brief moment she wanted nothing more than to lean into his hardness, feel his arms surround her. But giving into that temporary weakness wasn't going to stop what was sure to be starting even now.

"Evil," she said in a not-so-steady tone, "prefers the dark."

Chapter Nine

Sloan stepped up beside her. He put a hand on her arm. "Don't panic," he stated with quiet authority. "Generators and back ups in the city will have the lights back on any minute."

Moments later the electricity came back on. Briana sighed out a shaky exhale. Thank the Goddess for modern day amenities. Centuries ago a Demon attack would have been pulled off without any problem because of the controlled darkness. Just the thought of that fact sent shivers snaking through her. She frowned. Oddly enough, she felt ... calm instead of fearful. Why?

She looked from Sloan to Hunter, trying hard to determine their moods or thoughts. Hunter was frowning at Sloan. What was that all about? She followed his gaze and realized he was glaring at the hand Sloan still had on her arm. An out-of-place thrill of happiness careened through her. If she didn't know better, she'd swear Hunter wasn't happy about Sloan touching her. Then it occurred to her. Sloan's unruffled façade, his touch, was the reason she was feeling so calm. *How strange is that?* Confusion swamped her. She wasn't in the least bit attracted to him—handsome though he was—and she'd never had another human be able to calm her like that with just a touch. This revelation would need examining later.

But right now, she had a demon on the loose and too close for comfort.

"The lights coming back on will only slow him down a little," she stated, moving away from both men and going over to the window. She pushed the drapes back and looked out into the night's darkness.

"Who the hell are you talking about?" Hunter demanded. She could hear the mixed emotions of anger and—something else in his tone. Jealousy? "Damn, Briana, you're going to drive me crazy with all this."

Staring hard into the night, she suddenly saw a shadow slink across the street. Her heart raced alarmingly. Whatever this evil was, he was coming for her. She knew it with a certainty that settled deep. Chances were that he knew she was getting ready to search for the Sphere and he'd been sent to stop her. She had to do the Spell. Now. She swung back to face Hunter and Sloan.

"I wish I had more time to explain, to make you understand all this," she told them in a rush, "but I've ran out of time and options. I know you're not going to believe me, but there is an … evil outside right now. Most likely it's a demon. He's here to stop me from casting the Locating Spell. If he—" She paused and took a steady breath then released it. "If he gets to me, then everything is lost."

"First," Hunter gritted out roughly, "I don't care who or what is out there. He has to get past me before he ever reaches you." He spit out a few foul words. "Second, you're spouting pure nonsense and trying to distract us for some reason. You've already confessed to the thefts, Briana, so why this elaborate hoax? What the hell can you think to gain from it?"

Anger surged through her so hard and fast she nearly doubled over from the painfully stark force of it. That was the final straw. All the repressed emotions she'd been holding inside since the theft of the Sphere came rushing up from where she'd restrained them. She didn't even have to utter the spells aloud. They flew through her mind, a mental tirade of fury that threatened to make her lose complete control.

Countless objects around the room suddenly became airborne and went flying in all directions, crashing into walls, furniture, and even aiming at the two stunned men. A hard, fierce wind came out of nowhere and blew through the room, turning the flying objects into dangerous missiles. Hunter and Sloan were ducking and cussing at the same time.

"Briana, stop!" Hunter shouted. He lunged for her. Only Sloan made it there first. Pushing his brother aside, he grabbed her in his arms and held on.

Surprisingly, Briana felt comforting calm settle over her. *How the heck did he do that?* She blinked several times, and then forced her mind to stop the spells and chaos. Instant quiet blanketed the room.

Sloan slowly released her and took a step back. "Alright, now?"

She nodded and looked at Hunter. His handsome features were set in a mask of anger. She suddenly realized what he might be thinking. When he had touched her, her emotions were out of control. Sloan's touch calmed her. Hunter thought she responded to Sloan for an entirely different reason …

Sloan coughed out a strangled laugh. "Stop looking like a thundercloud, bro. I have no intention of trying to steal your woman."

Hunter growled at him. "Funny. She's not my woman. And you could have fooled me. You can't seem to keep your hands off her."

Hey, guys, did we forget that there is a demon on the prowl in the front yard? She was just as confused about this touching thing as Hunter was, but there were more important things to worry about right now.

"Think about it, Hunter," Sloan explained. "She obviously has telekinetic powers that are unbalanced by her emotions. That explains why something drastic happens every time she's upset or angry, or …" He gave her a quick grin before turning back to Hunter. "And you seem to cause those emotions to be out of control. Since she's obviously not attracted to me, then it stands to reason that I—or someone else—would be able to calm her—while you do the opposite."

"Okkaayy," Briana choked out in embarrassment. "She is standing right here. Stop talking about me like I'm some kind of strange object to dissect." She slapped her hands on her hips. "And it's not telekinetic powers! I'm so tired of you two being so stubborn about this."

"Stay calm, Briana," Sloan murmured. "No need to repeat your last stunt."

"Calm?" She barely managed to gain control of the surge of anger again. "I just told you we have a possible demon out there and you're concerned about who calms me and who arouses me? Men!"

One look at their stunned expressions and she immediately recalled what she'd just said. Arouses. She chewed on her bottom lip and closed her eyes for a moment. *Goddess help me, I can't take much more of this turmoil. Are you punishing me by bringing*

Hunter into my life at this time? I so don't need this.

Thankfully the two men had the decency not to mention her embarrassing goof. Too, it could have been because neither of them had the chance. The loud boom of the back door crashing open broke the strained silence between them. Hunter and Sloan glanced at each other, pulled their concealed guns from their jackets and then mouthed a silent "stay here" at her. They quickly hurried out of the room.

"Like heck I'm staying here," she muttered. She knew what had broken that door and she wasn't about to let them face this alone. Humans, despite being tough cops like Hunter and Sloan were, just didn't have what it took to confront and win against a demon.

She felt a moment of panic. *I just hope I have what it takes ... !*

Chapter Ten

She rushed out into the hall so fast she ran straight into Hunter's back. He shot a nasty glare at her and muttered low, "I should have known." She mockingly raised her brows at his scowl and mouthed, "You really didn't think I'd let you face a demon alone, did you?"

Hunter growled under his breath. He grabbed her by the shoulders and hauled her close against him. His mouth tickled her ear as he asked darkly, "Ever been spanked, Briana?"

She gasped as startling contradictions flooded her. The sane part of her realized he was actually threatening her. The woman in her reacted on a more basic level, desire instantly pooling low in her belly at the erotic visual that popped in her mind.

Sloan suddenly leaned into them both and whispered low, "Save it for another time, bro. Then, we'll team up. I'll hold her down and you can do the spanking." He mimicked Hunter's soft growl. "But right now we've got trouble with a capital T. I think I heard more than one intruder. Sounds like there are several more outside by the door."

Hunter snarled, "Stay back," at Briana before roughly pushing her behind them. Common sense told her to do as he said. They were cops and were trained to handle dangerous situations. And besides, she'd have a better chance at spell casting if she had a clear path straight to the enemy. She watched as Hunter and Sloan used hand motions to communicate as they maneuvered closer to the back door entrance. Hunter moved on silent tread to the left, and Sloan went to the right.

She took a deep breath and exhaled slowly, forcibly calming her senses. She had the bad feeling that their very lives were at stake if something went wrong and any spell she used misfired. She felt her power surge stronger with every calming breath she inhaled. She cleared her mind of all emotions.

> *Powers that Be,*
> *Send to me,*
> *Strength and might,*
> *And all power I need*
> *To win this fight.*

The words were barely past her lips when all hell broke loose. As one, a huge black mass of bodies surged into the opened back door. Briana choked out a small cry. There were more than just a few—the mass had to contain at least ten demons. As soon as they were inside, they separated into individual beings, half flying into Hunter, the other half into Sloan.

Raising her hands, she managed to hit the last two separating from the group with a disintegrating spell. Their dying screams pierced her ears, nearly bringing her to her knees. She straightened and saw globs of foul smelling liquid pool on the floor where they had stood. Wrinkling her nose she moved closer, trying to pick out more bodies to hit.

Hunter and Sloan were firing their guns, but the bullets were going right through the demons. Within seconds both men dropped their weapons and started throwing punches. The horrendous fighting sounds of bodies colliding, fists connecting, cries and howls of pain and anger, were deafening and beyond frightening. Briana's heart almost stopped. How could two mortals win in a fight against demons?

She slammed a disintegrating spell into the backs of the demons closest to her, lessening Hunter's adversaries by two. She swung to Sloan and did the same. Frantic she tried to aim for the remaining ones but was afraid she would hit one of the men and that caused her to hesitate. She closed her eyes and whispered a heart-felt prayer to the Goddess for help.

Opening her eyes again she suddenly realized that both men were somehow pushing their opponents back, throwing punches so hard and so fast, their fists were blurs. Their mortal strength wasn't as strong as the demons' but it was keeping the fiends off balance. Fascinated she watched as Hunter and Sloan fought like demons themselves, almost in perfect sync with their defensive moves. Gradually they began to force the remaining demons, as one bulk, back into the center of the hall. The demons collided, slamming into the ones behind them and falling into a chaotic, tangled mass. Hunter and Sloan jumped clear, and Hunter shouted out the command,

"Now, Briana!"

She didn't hesitate. She struck with every ounce of power she had in her.

Electrical, magical, incredibly forceful power surged from her raised hands, striking with deadly accuracy. A huge blast exploded the demons into a mass of flying body parts, splattering gore, and fading, ear-splitting screeches.

Suddenly drained, Briana slumped to the floor. Eerie silence blanketed the room. A myriad of emotions flowed through her, mixing with the complete exhaustion that always came from using too much power at one time. Relief swamped her. They had survived and destroyed the demons.

Trepidation hit her then, much harder than the other vying emotions. She was too exhausted now. What if those demons were only the first of an army ready to attack? How would she be able to do the Spell now—before it was too late? For one brief moment she wanted to cry; the tears burned her throat, then her eyes. But then she resolutely straightened her shoulders, raised her head, and looked right into Hunter's eyes.

She lost her breath. Never in all her life would she have ever expected to see a man look at her like he was doing then. His dark blue-grey eyes smoldered, searing her with a look of passionate heat and—something else she wasn't quite sure of.

He slowly crossed the space between them, his gaze never releasing hers. When he reached her, he leaned down and grasped her by the waist, lifting her. She fell against his hard chest, bracing herself with her hands and pushing back. She barely had a moment to whisper his name before his mouth came crushing down on hers.

He swallowed her soft cry, roughly devouring her mouth, and stealing what breath she had left. She instantly melted into him and he tightened his arms around her, melding their bodies together in the most intimate of embraces.

Despite needing to breathe she returned his kiss, opening her mouth to the insistence of his tongue pushing against the seam of her lips. When their tongues met, the lustful heat swamping her made her knees buckle. Lucky for her, he was holding her tight enough to keep her from falling.

She would have willingly died right there in his possessive hold, with his mouth devouring hers in a kiss she wanted to go on forever, and just forget the rest of the world. That's if it hadn't been for Sloan's sarcastic remark.

"Well, damn. I thought that only happened in movies."

Hunter released her mouth, choking on a laugh at the same time. Breathless and now completely confused, she stared at him. His handsome features were still darkened with passion, but there was a strange glint in his eyes now that hadn't been there before. *Huh?*

Hunter grinned at Sloan. "I just figured I'd be a lot safer if I was kissing her, than you would be standing over there, once her emotions took over and turned that demon blob into a missile." He chuckled before pressing a quick hard kiss on her open mouth, and then murmured wickedly, "And, hell, kissing her was a lot—uh— more decent than what I really wanted to do."

"Is this where I say, 'hey bro, I'm too young to hear that kind of talk'?" Sloan shook his head and laughed too. He looked around the hall, sobering instantly. "Man, did this really happen?"

Briana couldn't get her brain to work fast enough to say anything. Hunter's hot gaze stayed locked with hers and she tried to remember that breathing was a good thing. She was still trying to digest what he'd just said. Had she only heard what she wanted to hear?

Then, she realized what else he'd said. She blinked rapidly several times, breaking free from his captive stare. "You said demons. You believe me now."

Hunter closed his eyes for a long moment. He opened them and then slowly released the tight hold he still had on her, his arms hanging loosely around her waist. "Yeah, I believe you. I don't have much of a choice, do I." He looked at the gory mess still bubbling in a black puddle on the floor. "Never in a million years," he muttered, shaking his head. "But it's kind of hard not to believe when you're getting the hell beat out of you by a bunch of straight-out-of-a-nightmare demons."

Briana gasped. She pushed away from him, her gaze thoroughly sweeping over him. "You were hurt! Why didn't you say something!" There wasn't a place on him that didn't have a splat of blood, either from his own wounds or from the demons', and his skin was bruised and scratched in multiple places. One quick glance at Sloan confirmed he was in the same shape.

"We're fine," Hunter muttered. "Thanks to your magical sharp-shooting. And Sloan and I work great as a team; we've never been bested in a fight yet." He suddenly groaned when her wandering hands pushed up his torn shirt to roam over his bruised chest. "Briana, give me some mercy here. Stop touching me like that." He grabbed her hands and clasped them in one of his. Then he grasped her chin with his other hand and lifted her face to look into her eyes. "We've got a serious situation here, sweetheart. You've got a lot of explaining to do, and we've got to get this mess cleaned before Mom gets home. I don't want her involved in any of this."

Before he'd removed her hands from his chest, she'd felt his all-male response to her touch and it thrilled her, instantly pooling desire straight to the lower part of her belly. And he still had that strange, hot glint in his eyes. A sudden weakness swamped her. *Oh yeah. Breathe. Don't think about that look in his eyes.* And he was right. This wasn't the time for thoughts like that …

"I don't have the spare energy to clean it magically," she said, indicating the bubbling glob. "But between the three of us, we should be able to dispose of it quickly."

"What the hell do you do with a gory mess like that?" Sloan muttered. He pulled out a broom and dustpan from the hall closet, and Hunter opened a box of large, plastic lawn bags. Making faces, scrunching their noses at the God-awful smell, and muttering cuss words under their breaths, the two men efficiently cleaned the floor and managed to get all the glob mass into the bags. Briana was still feeling a bit weak, so she stood to the side and watched.

She couldn't help it. She just had to comment. "It's not every day a woman gets to watch two men clean up a mess they made."

Hunter slanted a wicked grin at her. "Careful, sweetheart. You're already in serious trouble. Adding to the list isn't a smart thing to do."

She grinned back, unrepentant. "I'm not afraid of you, Hunter."

"Famous last words."

"Time out," Sloan admonished, his tone turning serious. "Briana, will it be safe to just dump this in the garbage bin? Or should we burn it or something?"

She shook her head. She blinked hard several times, trying to clear the odd mist in front of her eyes. Where had that come from? "I zapped it with a huge surge of magic. It should be completely neutralized." *I hope.*

Hunter handed the bulky bags to Sloan, his eyes on Briana. Under his breath he murmured, "I think she needs to sit down." He moved across the space between them with predatory speed and managed to catch her up in his arms just as she felt the world spin and turn dark.

Briana had the brief thought to hope that she hadn't spoken the words aloud when she felt the black void swallow her just as Hunter lifted her in his strong arms: *I love your arms around me, Hunter ...*

Chapter Eleven

"Splash her face with the water, Hunter. Stop being so damn gentle."

"Do it," Briana muttered as she came fully awake, "And I'll turn you into something distasteful."

She heard Hunter chuckle. "Welcome back."

She sat up, carefully, and counted to ten to give the world a chance to stop spinning around her. She was lying in Hunter's lap, and he was sitting on the sofa. Sloan was leaning over her with a large pitcher of water. She shot a warning glare at him and he quickly backed off.

Hunter helped her settle back against his chest. "What happened, Briana? Do you usually faint after using so much magic?"

"I'm just as confused as you are." It was a first for her. Usually, she was left feeling a bit drained after using a large amount of magic at one time, but she'd never fainted. Her mind flew back over the battle sequence, pulling up every little detail. Right before she'd zapped the demons, she'd been watching as Hunter and Sloan maneuvered them into position. She recalled feeling very impressed. And a bit … aroused. Watching Hunter fight so skillfully, so ferociously, had aroused her! How sick was that! And then, instead of her emotions being completely out of control the arousal had strengthened her magic and the spell had hit its mark with deadly accuracy. The tremendous strength of the spell had zapped her energy force.

Sloan suddenly grinned, quickly covering his mouth to keep a chuckle from escaping. Looking into his eyes, she knew he'd just come to the same conclusion she had. "One word, and you're a dead man," she threatened silkily. As it was, she felt Hunter stiffen behind her and knew he'd probably just put two and two together and come up with the same answer. She shook her head. It was definite now: the Goddess had to be punishing her for losing the Sphere. Putting Hunter in her life at this crucial point was just what she so didn't need.

She sat up and pushed away from Hunter. "I have to do the Location Spell as soon as possible. Things are getting out of control."

"It's definitely past time for explanations," Hunter said, his tone abruptly no-nonsense now. "Start talking, Briana, and don't leave out any details."

Fine. The sooner she told them, the sooner she could get the Spell done. She gave them a brief history lesson on the Sphere, and then explained, "My ancestors sacrificed their lives to place a powerful magic spell on the miniature living willow tree. Then it was sealed in the unbreakable Sphere. As long as it's kept and guarded by the descendent of the original ancestors, the Tree will live. And as long as the Tree lives, the main door to the Underworld will remain closed. I'm the direct descendent and it's been my duty to protect the Sphere all my life.

"A little over a month ago the unthinkable happened. One moment the Sphere was in my possession ... and then it suddenly disappeared. Poof. Gone in a split second. You know the rest of this story. My emotions were out of control and I accidentally burned the house down with a Spell—thus losing all my craft tools. I was afraid to openly purchase the objects I needed to do a Locating Spell because if—whomever—stole the Sphere were still nearby then he or she would know what I was doing and would stop me. I don't know how powerful the enemy is and I couldn't take the chance of being defeated. I had to do everything under stealth and complete secrecy." She stopped to glare at them. "I had every intention of returning those items. I was only borrowing them for a short time."

"Right." Sloan slumped over in the chair he had dropped into once she started her story. "And you couldn't ask for help? I'm sorry, Briana, but committing theft is a crime no matter what the reason. Damn it, you could have come to me after you moved in with mom. I could have offered some kind of protection while you did what you had to do."

"Of course, Sloan," Briana scoffed. "You would have believed me instantly and helped. Why didn't I think of that?"

"This Location Spell," Hunter interrupted smoothly, "It will find—and bring the Sphere back to you?"

She shook her head. "It will tell me where to search for it, but nothing more." She sighed. "For someone to be able to steal it from me like that, they would have to be incredibly powerful and knowledgeable. This enemy's skills would be unlike any other I've come across. I will have to locate the Sphere and then figure out a way to steal it back." She shifted in his arms, tension building in her with the thought. "And time is running out. The Tree can only live so long without being in my possession. If I don't find it—very soon—then all Hell will be released. That door will open. And the demons you fought today will seem like sweet little kittens compared to what will come out."

Goddess help them all. "I have to do the Spell. Now."

"No way in hell," Hunter grit out, his jaw clenching. "I'm not going to let you go off searching for some hell-spawn with powers strong enough to kill anything or anyone in his path. Think again, Briana. There has to be another way."

Fury surged from deep within her. Hadn't he heard a word she'd said? What more would it take to make him realize just how 'life-and-death-world-ending' serious this situation was? "You're not going to let me?" She pushed his arms away and stood up, visibly shaking with the volatile emotion swamping her. She didn't want to decipher why his attitude was making her so angry, so frustrated, when she should have been thrilled at his protectiveness. She looked him straight in the eyes and stated softly yet firmly, her threat obvious. "Try and stop me, Hunter."

She walked out of the room, head high, shoulders straight, and her voice dangerously calm. "I can be just as deadly as my enemy. No one will stop me from doing what I have to do. No one."

She didn't stay to hear what he might have said. She marched up the stairs with determined strides to her bedroom, all the while trying to calm down. He was an intelligent man; why then couldn't he understand the horrifying ramifications of the situation? Fighting a mass of demons hadn't convinced him this wasn't some crazy hoax? She wanted to hate him for his purposeful determination to make this into something more logical that he could handle. But she couldn't. She admired his steely strength. She just wished she could have counted on him ...

She retrieved the borrowed items needed for the Spell from her closet and carried them down to the basement. Part of her knew she had to stay calm and think only about the Spell and finding the Sphere. But the other part of her remained furious with Hunter. And hurt. Even after all that had happened, he still doubted the real truth. And he doubted her. He thought he could simply tell her to forget it all, and she'd obey. That hurt most of all. Maybe some small part of him accepted now that she was a witch, but he wasn't seeing the full picture, the real person. And she'd been vulnerable enough to believe he was starting to care about her. Did the man go around kissing other women like he did her?

Stop thinking about him. She had priorities right now and Hunter's macho ego wasn't one of the things she wanted to deal with. She grimaced. *Now or never!*

She put all the items on the floor in the center of the magic circle she had painted on the wood flooring. Tall, white candles rimmed the edge of the circle and with a flick of her hand she lit them. The sweet smell of lavender and sage instantly filled the room. She breathed in the familiar scents, pulling them deep into her lungs. She exhaled a calming breath and began to relax the rest of her tense body. Mentally, she started at the bottom of her feet, sending calming waves of warmth into every inch of her body until she reached the top of her head. Satisfied with the calmness indicating all her chakras were opened, she waved her hand over her body and disposed of her clothes. Naked, she stepped into the circle.

One by one, she spell-casted each item as she placed it in the copper pot. Barely discernable sparks of glittering lights danced from her hands to her fingers and then visibly melded with each tool. The candle flames flared higher with each word of her soft-spoken chant.

> *Powers that Be,*
> *Attune to me.*
> *Bless these tools for their purpose be,*
> *Help them show me what I need to see.*
> *Show me the path of my destiny,*
> *Show me the path where I need to be.*

Waving her hand over the now full pot of items, she whispered the ancient incantation for the Location Spell. The Gaelic words flowed naturally from her, sounding like a soft wave rushing to the shore. With each repeat, the wave became stronger, and her voice louder.

A loud, roaring wind rushed forth from the four corners of the basement room. It swirled around the circle, though never touched it. Faster and faster it spun, soon bringing everything in its path into a blurring whirlwind that pulsated with countless bright colors.

Now! She had to say the final words that would complete the Spell.

The basement door burst open. Briana stumbled in her words, and stared in shock at Hunter and Sloan as they rushed into the room. Their running sprint caused them to immediately fall forward into the whirlwind. *No!* This couldn't be happening! Not now. Not at this moment ...

"Briana, stop!" Hunter didn't hesitate. He jumped forward into the circle with her. Behind him, Sloan yelled a cuss word and followed him in. The momentum of the swirling wind shoved him into Briana, with Sloan slamming into them both at the same time.

... At the exact same moment her emotions for Hunter flew out of control and unable to stop—she uttered the crucial final words of the Spell:

"To that destination, Fate, take me."

The clap of thunder was ear splitting. The swirling blackness was nauseating. The ferocious swirling wind was skin burning.

Briana's scream was heartbreaking.

Chapter Twelve

Various conflicting thoughts bombarded her the moment the black mist cleared her vision. Briana blinked hard several times, but couldn't comprehend what she was seeing ... and feeling.

The sweet-smelling hay beneath her naked body wasn't as comfortable as she thought it was supposed to be. She was sure she'd read that romantic notion somewhere. There were several sharp points poking in countless places under her back, butt, and legs and she was sure she'd have scratches all over.

Despite that, all she could really think about was the naked man lying on top of her.

Hunter.

She blinked again and looked up into his dark blue-grey eyes. Their faces were mere inches apart and his shoulder length hair fell forward onto her cheeks. Their bodies were aligned in all the right spots ...

And she was sure that all she had to do was take one very deep inhale and his hot, hard erection would easily slip right inside her waiting body.

Hunter's hot breath wafted over her lips. "I could get used to this," he murmured sexily. "Having you naked on top of me, or beneath me, every time you try a spell."

The Spell! What happened? Briana gasped, her lust instantly turning into fear. "This can't be happening." She somehow got her hands wedged between their bodies and pushed him. "Get off me, Hunter. This is serious."

"Oomph," Hunter muttered with a pained grimace as her knee accidentally connected with his lower groin. "Easy, Briana. Stop moving for a second and let me get some semblance of—control here. Damn, you drive me crazy. Stay still!" He grabbed her hands and shoved them above her head, locking onto her wrists with one of his hands. He reached down and grabbed her hip with his other hand and applied enough pressure to force her to stop struggling. "Calm down. And don't you dare utter one word of a spell right now."

"Hunter!" She cringed at the frantic tone of her voice but darn it, this was serious. "Something went wrong. You shouldn't be—here." *Wherever here is!* "I have to find out what happened with the Spell."

"I'm not letting you up until you calm down," he stated, his voice oddly husky. "And not until I can safely get up too."

"Safely?" She shoved up with her body. "Now, who's driving who crazy? We don't even know what happened and you're worrying about—oh my Goddess."

She barely had time to finish when Hunter met her thrust with a very intimate one of his own. His shaft pressed hard and insistent against her bare center and he dropped his full weight on her. She stilled, breath caught in her throat, and her heart racing so fast and hard she was sure he could hear it. Never mind where here was. Right now all she could think about was the hard, aggressive body draped over hers. He felt so good. Heat pooled low, close to where their bodies touched in the most intimate spot.

"Breathe with me, sweetheart," Hunter muttered with a part desperate, part sexy growl, "Don't think of anything else right now. Just breathe." He groaned, the sound making his chest rumble against her breasts. "Now's the time to stay calm, baby. That's it. Let your body relax."

She somehow managed to do as he said and forced a calm—she was far from feeling—into her mind and body. As soon as she relaxed she felt Hunter trying to do the same. She watched the myriad of emotions cross his handsome features as his breath sloughed roughly between his lips and he kept his eyes closed tight. His look of strained passion almost had her breathing erratically all over again.

Finally he sighed out a rough groan and dropped his forehead to rest against hers. "One of these days we're going to have to follow this through, baby." He slowly lifted his head and opened his eyes. "But, you're right. Now isn't the time. We need to find out what just happened."

He rolled off her and stood in one graceful lunge. Then he reached down and caught her hands to help her up. Briana made the valiant effort to look anywhere but at his naked body. She could still feel the imprint of every hard inch of him on her shaking body. The man was just too sexy for his own good. *Goddess help me.*

"Where the hell are we?" Hunter took a thorough look around. "And where is Sloan? He was right behind me before that—whatever that hellish wind was—sucked us in."

Briana looked around. They were in some kind of barn. The roof was at least two stories high, and the building was made of rough-cut wood. There were haystacks in every corner, various odd looking tools, and several empty stalls. The air smelled musty and old. If it hadn't been for the freshness of the haystacks, she'd have sworn no one had been here for a very long time.

Where had the Spell transported them? An old ranch or farm, maybe somewhere outside Inverness city limits? And what did this place have to do with finding the Sphere? Her thoughts flew in countless different directions. Maybe the Sphere was hidden here? *Please let that be the answer ...*

Her heart raced. To heck with calm. This was just a little more than even she wanted to accept. "Maybe the Location Spell brought me here instead of just showing me where the Sphere is."

Before either of them could say anything else, a loud commotion at the barn doors caused them to turn and stare at a sight—that might have been comical if it hadn't been so ... odd.

A naked Sloan stumbled into the barn, cussing up a blue streak. Right behind him was a woman holding a long, wooden pitchfork and poking it at him every time he stopped moving.

Briana politely ignored Sloan's nakedness. And besides, it was the woman who had her full attention. She heard Hunter mutter, "What the hell?" and nodded her head at his assessment. They obviously weren't in Inverness anymore.

At least, not in the same time period they'd been in before the Spell.

The woman was dressed in a straight, floor length dress shift of pale green, long sleeved, square necked, and oddly medieval-looking. Noticeably lovely, her heart shaped face had a few scattered freckles across cameo skin, a cupid-bow mouth, and her lashes and brows were the same deep red as her long curly hair.

Briana took in a sharp inhale of air, realization stunning her. Not only was the woman strangely dressed, but she also had a strange aura around her. If she didn't know better, she'd swear the woman was a witch. An odd glow of power appeared to circle her. Briana relaxed a little. *At least her aura is pastel and not black.* And she didn't exactly feel any kind of threat coming from her. That had to be a good thing, right?

"*C'o a tha thu?*"

The woman's question was filled with menace as she stared at them, keeping the pitchfork aimed at Sloan.

Gaelic. Briana choked back a gasp. "She's speaking Gaelic."

"What did she say?" Hunter asked.

"She wants to know who we are."

"Right back at you," Hunter muttered. "I want answers. As in yesterday."

"Don't anger her any more than she already is, Hunter," Sloan cautioned with a backward glance at the woman. "She knows how to use that damn thing."

Briana's thoughts were flying. Why was the woman dressed like that and speaking Gaelic? This couldn't bode well, no matter what the answer was. She cleared a throat gone dry and said, "'*s mise Briana. C'o a tha thu?*"

After a slight hesitation, the woman answered. "Kassidy." Her eyes narrowed as she studied Briana more closely. *I was right,* Briana thought. It wasn't hard for witches to recognize their own kind, and she could see the sudden comprehension in the woman's hazel eyes.

Kassidy lowered the pitchfork—although not before sending Sloan a nasty glare, and then raised her hands toward them. Before Briana could warn them she was about to spell cast, Kassidy uttered the words and a spark of brilliant light lit the barn's interior. Just as fast as it had appeared, it was gone.

"There," Kassidy announced, "We'll be able to understand each other now."

Briana glanced at Hunter and Sloan's confused expressions. "She's a witch. She just used a translation spell so that no matter what language is spoken, the one hearing the words will hear it in their own language, and be able to speak the other's language too."

"Now, let's start over," Kassidy's lilting Scottish accent was strong but her words were perfect English cadence. "Who are you, and what are you doing here?"

Hunter shifted next to Briana, then muttered in a low voice, "This conversation would be a lot easier if Sloan and I weren't buck naked. Do something, please."

It took a lot of effort, but Briana managed to hold back her grin and not laugh. "I noticed you didn't say anything about *my* nakedness. I'm not sure if I should be offended or complimented."

Hunter gave her a quick, wicked smile so sexy all her senses went into overdrive. "Trust me, baby. It was definitely a compliment." He lowered his voice and the sensual tone hummed over her like hot honey. "I like you naked."

Okay. That comment wasn't going to help get him clothed any time soon! Face flushing, she looked at Kassidy. "Um. Could you spell us some clothes?"

Kassidy's eyebrows rose in curious question. "Was I wrong? You *are* a witch?"

Briana nodded her head, embarrassment flooding her. "Yes, but I'm a bit handicapped at certain times." She glanced at Hunter and he grinned knowingly. "And this happens to be one of those times." Oh, how she was going to get even with him for purposely using her reactions to him against her.

Kassidy waved her hands and they were instantly clothed. Albeit, not in the clothes they expected. Briana ran her hands over the floor length dress that resembled what Kassidy was wearing. It was in a lovely pale pink, soft linen, and was very form fitting around her slender waist and hips, and nicely tight under her breasts, pushing them up. Sans bra and yet it looked as though she was wearing one. The long sleeves were wide cuffed at the wrist, hanging loosely. And the shoes on her feet were some kind of soft leather, resembling ballerina slippers. She smiled, smoothing her hand over the dress again; she could easily get used to this free-flowing gown. It reminded her of the V-lined, silk gowns she wore during certain ceremonies.

Beside her Hunter grumbled low and nasty under his breath. She looked up and had just a split moment of clarity to realize that laughing was not the thing to do right then. The thundercloud expression on his handsome features was priceless.

Tight, black leather pants molded to his muscled legs and thighs. His black boots were almost knee high and appeared to be of the sturdiest leather. The white shirt he was wearing closely resembled the pirate shirts she remembered seeing in old movies; wide loose sleeves, low-cut front that exposed his strong chest down to a V, and laced strings instead of buttons. She hid her grin as butterflies danced in her stomach. The entire ensemble somehow worked on him. It made him look incredibly virile, predatory, and oh-so-sexy male.

"Oh wow," she murmured.

Hunter cussed. "If you laugh, you're dead. What the hell is this?"

Looking quite sincere, Kassidy vigorously shook her head. "Oh no, definitely nothing in Hell. This is the proper clothing for here." Before Hunter could reply, Sloan uttered a cuss word so nasty, Briana and Kassidy blanched. Tone dripping sarcasm, he stared at Kassidy and demanded, "What, no shirt for me?"

Kassidy smiled, her eyes dancing with obvious mischief. "Oh. Sorry. I must not have been thinking clearly." She waved her hand and a shirt identical to Hunter's instantly appeared on Sloan.

Sloan stomped over to Hunter. "Damn it, we're not even wearing underwear under these ridiculous outfits. I think she's playing with us, Hunter." He shot a glare at Kassidy and muttered, "Smart assed witch."

"Sloan!" Briana hit him on the arm. The last thing she needed was her 'calm connection' to be out of control. She had the uneasy feeling she was going to need Sloan's calmness before too much longer. Despite her purposeful 'I'm-in-control' look, she was actually shaking inside, scared and worried. But she couldn't let them see that. Just for good measure she slugged Sloan again. "Will you just shut up until I can find out what's going on here? And in case you've forgotten ... witches have powers you don't. Are you really that brave to keep being so nasty to her until we find out if she's friend or foe?"

He growled low. "She stuck me with that damn pitchfork. Right in a—vulnerable spot—deliberately. It wasn't my fault I ended up naked and lying on top of her. Damn woman didn't even give me a chance to try and explain."

"In my defense, I thought he was attacking me." Kassidy glared back at Sloan.

Briana turned to Hunter. "Help."

Hunter frowned at Kassidy, but nonetheless smartly cautioned Sloan to shut up for a few minutes. Relieved, Briana sighed, rubbing at her forehead. Her head was beginning to ache with all the chaotic thoughts running around inside. Her first priority—the very thing at the center of this situation—was to find out where the Sphere was and why the Spell had brought them here.

"Where are we, Kassidy? You spoke Gaelic at first, and you have a Scottish accent now."

Kassidy chewed on her lip before answering. "You must have used a transportation spell to get here, right? But why?" She studied them closer. Her eyes narrowed again and she took a few steps back toward the open barn doors. "If you used a spell, then you have to know this is Inverness-da." She took a deep breath and exhaled in a puff laced with obvious fear. Her next words shook Briana to the depths of her soul.

"You are in the parallel world of Inverness, Florida. This is the Scottish side of the veil."

Chapter Thirteen

Briana sank down on the nearest hay bale, and willed her heart to slow down. "How can this have happened? I worded the Location Spell with the precise words it needed." She looked up at Hunter and frowned angrily. "This is all your fault. If you hadn't tried to be so macho wanting to stop me, I'd have completed the Spell correctly."

Hunter stomped over to her. "Macho? Just because I didn't like the idea of you chasing off after some kind of demon madman, you call my concern macho? Fine. Next time I'll just let you go off unprotected, and save myself the consequences—like being in this damn crazy situation now."

"Your interference may have cost me everything," Briana grit out. She had to blame someone. She didn't want to accept the truth, that she was responsible for this mess now. Thanks to her ineptness. *I will not cry about this.* Instead she muttered, "Go away, Hunter. I can't even think straight with you around me right now."

He grasped her upper arms and hauled her to her feet and up against his chest. Almost nose-to-nose, he snarled. "Damn it, you little witch. I'm more than willing to go home and leave you to your unbalanced world. Send Sloan and me back now." He gave her a little shake and then groaned. "Hell, I can't believe I'm accepting this so easily. Demon enemies, misfiring witches who can't control their own powers, and … parallel worlds! How nightmare-in-hell insane is this?" He shoved her away and turned his back on her for a long minute, breathing roughly.

Briana's heart stuttered. An angry Hunter she could handle. But a confused one wasn't something she was sure she could deal with. He was a strong man, highly intelligent, a man who would never accept defeat easily. He fought his battles with the steely determination that he would win every time. He commanded control. And in one brief moment she had turned his entire life upset down without giving him the chance to fight back.

"I'm sorry," she whispered, her voice breaking. "Give me a little time to figure all this out and I can get you and Sloan back home."

"If you're here for the reason I think you are," Kassidy interrupted, "then time isn't something you have to spare. *Tha iad a` tighinn.*"

They are coming.

Briana shot a fearful glance to the barn doors. "Who?"

Kassidy's lovely face was creased in worry and fear. "The ones who will stop at nothing to keep you from your goal."

Briana knew she was taking a chance but some inner instinct told her Kassidy knew everything. "Do you know where the Sphere is, Kassidy?"

"I have it."

"What!" Briana grasped her by the arm. "Give it to me! You have to know I'm the rightful guardian and only I can keep it safe. Where is it? Stop stalling, Kassidy, give me the Sphere now!"

"I don't have it here with me. And we need to talk about this before I give it back."

Briana had always heard the expression 'seeing red' referring to when you got so angry you couldn't think straight. She experienced it now. An instant red haze nearly blinded her for a moment. Nevertheless, her voice was deadly calm as she looked into Kassidy's wide eyes and stated, "I will not tell you again."

"Threatening me won't get the Sphere back in your hands any quicker," Kassidy stated, her tone hard. "There is much that needs to be dealt with, despite the dire loss of time." She glanced over her shoulder to the open doors. "We must hurry. Dark is nigh and they are coming. I can hear them close."

"Who is coming?" Hunter demanded. He and Sloan moved to the doors and cautiously checked around, peering out into the descending darkness of evening. After a few moments Hunter nodded to Sloan. "I can hear approaching footsteps." He turned back to Kassidy. "Who are we talking about? An enemy? Armed? Damn. Our guns didn't transport with us."

Sloan grunted. "Damn that you didn't even stutter when saying that."

"Yeah, I know. Scares the hell out of me how easily I'm accepting this crap."

"Same here, bro. I shouldn't be this calm."

Briana hid her smile. Despite the out-of-this-world-unbelievable circumstances, both men were taking it moment by moment, their natural fighting instincts coming into play at the threat of an enemy. If she could get the Sphere, work out a returning Spell and transport them home, then all this would simply seem like a weird dream. And just maybe … Hunter would forgive her for this fiasco. And just maybe … they might have the time to explore the growing attraction between them to a fuller level. Her heart stuttered. Chances were Hunter wouldn't want to have anything to do with her now.

Kassidy hurried to the barn doors. "Help me close them. There is no time to leave now."

When the doors were closed, she stepped back and raised her hands in the air. Ancient Gaelic words preceded the whoosh of power that shot out of her. A nearly visible wave of iridescent colors flew around the room, coating the doors, the walls, the high ceiling. When the faint coat faded, seeming to sink into the wood structure, she shakily exhaled and sunk to the ground.

"We'll have to stay here tonight. But the warding spell will keep them from entering. They will see it as a place of no interest and go on."

"Sloan, help her over here to this haystack." Briana waved her hand and materialized a blanket. She spread it over the hay. "Witches are left feeling drained after using a huge amount of power. She'll need to rest for a few minutes."

Sloan lifted Kassidy up into his arms and carried her over to where Briana waited. He carefully placed her down then stepped back. His features were a mix of anger and frustration. "You're going to explain why the warding spell and who the hell you're afraid of, aren't you? Start talking lady; this is getting crazier by the minute and I'm not liking it."

"Sloan, come here," Hunter called out from his position at the barn doors, his voice a low rough whisper. He was looking out through a crack in the large wood slats. Briana followed him over but Hunter put an arm around her waist and pulled her back as Sloan stepped up to peek out the crack.

"What is it?" She didn't like the feeling she was getting. Hunter was in his protective mode, she could feel the steely strength of his grip and the stiff way he was holding his body. Fear crept through her. Whatever Kassidy was afraid of, was out there now. And it didn't bode well that even Hunter was unnerved.

Sloan stiffened. He glanced at them over his shoulder and mouthed the word "Hell."

Hunter pulled Briana farther back and the three of them moved over to where Kassidy sat on the blanket. His features were dark, his lips set in a thin line of anger.

"What the hell are those creatures?" he demanded, turning on Kassidy.

"Demon shifters."

The words shot horror through her and Briana stopped short of seeking safety in Hunter's arms. Kassidy's voice had been filled with something close to terror when she'd uttered them.

"Explain," Hunter bit out tersely, "and don't leave out any details. How do we fight something like that?"

"I don't know of any way to fight them," Kassidy answered, her hazel eyes dark and worried-filled. "Yet. But my warding spells seem to keep them away."

"What did they look like?" Briana asked Hunter. She'd never heard of demon shifters. She shuddered again. What else could go wrong at this point? *I don't think I want to know ...*

Hunter frowned. "They were walking upright like men, dressed like men, but their faces and limbs were—animalistic. There were about ten of them; some resembled bears, some wolves, and some looked like cats."

"Shapeshifters." Like witches and other preternatural beings, shapeshifters were believed to be only myth. Even though she'd never seen one, Briana knew they were real.

"No," Kassidy said. "Not exactly shapeshifters. They are actual demons that have possessed a human body. Once they take over the body, they begin to slowly morph. I thought at first they were to become shifters but their morphing has only progressed to their faces and limbs and it's been a gradual process. It's almost as though they are turning into real animals—with demon souls and human bodies. I haven't been able to figure out the purpose."

"Is there a master demon controlling them?" Briana shuddered at the thought. A master that powerful would be dangerous beyond comprehension.

Kassidy nodded her head. "He is an incredibly powerful being. I don't know where he is but he's made his presence known in the village and at the castle. Then, demon shifters started showing up a little over a month ago. They come only after dark, and usually attack only once per night. That's an oddity I'm still trying to understand too. I never know where they will show up, so I haven't been able to protect everyone. I'm draining my strength just keeping the castle warded."

"What do they do when they attack?" Sloan asked.

Kassidy cringed, her face paling. "They're ... carnivorous. They swarm in, isolate someone, then attack. After the ... feeding ... they disappear."

"Has anyone tried to kill them?" Hunter's frown deepened. "I can't believe no one would fight back."

"An insidious fear—unlike any that can be explained—grips the heart and immobilizes anyone in the vicinity where they show up. The fear is debilitating, it freezes you."

"This isn't good," Briana murmured, wrapping her arms around her waist as she shivered. "In order to be able to do that, their master would have to have powers beyond anything I've ever heard of. He would have to be able to control the demons and the people at the same time."

Kassidy sighed shakily. "He's strong enough to believe he has the power to open the door to hell."

Chapter Fourteen

"I'm sorry, bro."

Hunter turned away from his post by the door crack and stretched. He shook his head. "You didn't know." He ran a hand through his hair. "Hell, who would have ever imagined this?"

Sloan grunted. "Months ago my biggest problem was trying to keep the teenagers out of the lake at night. Damn kids insisted on swimming there despite that family of gators calling the place home."

Hunter grinned at the thought, but sobered just as quick. "I wonder if Inverness-da has alligators?" Just saying the name of the alternate world they were in now made the surge of anger he was holding back resurface. Resolutely he pushed it back. There wasn't any sense in letting it simmer. Despite the unbelievable probability of it, the truth was that they were in circumstances as real as anything. Instead of ranting at the impossibility, they needed to assess the situation and then deal with it.

Even though Kassidy had assured them the warding spell would last the night, he and Sloan had decided to stand guard. No sense in allowing the enemy an unprotected moment to strike. He just wished their weapons had transported with them; he felt a little naked without his gun.

"So," Sloan sat down and leaned back against one of the barn doors. It had to be past midnight but both of them were awake and alert. "What do we do next?"

Hunter thought back over the information Kassidy had told them earlier. Inverness-da was the parallel world of their own city, yet it was different in many ways. Here, they didn't have the modern weapons or knowledge of them, and their lives were simple—as though they had been frozen in a time from some past Scottish history. Witches and sorcerers, monsters in the night, were easily accepted as part of their reality in some old fashioned sense of superstition.

But the biggest difference was that here was where one of the main doors to Hell sat hidden.

And just as Briana's ancestors had guarded the Sphere, Kassidy's had protected the door.

Hunter sat down beside Sloan. He stretched out his legs. "At least this damn leather is soft and moves smoothly with you." He grimaced. He felt like some kind of medieval pirate.

Sloan chuckled. "It could have been worse. With the Scottish connection to this place, we could have ended up wearing kilts."

Hunter groaned. "Bite your tongue. And don't ever say that aloud around Briana. Put the thought in her head and we're doomed."

Sloan shook his head. "Witches," he muttered. "Never in a million years would I have believed we'd end up in a place like this and at the mercy of two witches. One has the power to dress us any way she wants, and the other has the power to turn the world upside down with just a wayward thought. I'm not ready for this, bro."

Hunter agreed with Sloan. Nothing in his life could have prepared him for this. He exhaled roughly. "After what Kassidy said, it looks like our main goal is to figure out how to stop that sorcerer from opening the door. How to stop him is going to be the hard part. He's obviously preparing for a war against Kassidy's side. We might as well accept that we're in for a fight, Sloan. We can't let those beasts we saw tonight reign free, or allow that damn sorcerer the chance to ever come back." For the umpteenth time he wished he had his gun. "Once Briana has the Sphere again, she can help Kassidy with the magic to permanently seal the door."

"That's if we can keep Briana calm."

"Yeah. Her emotions have ranged from one extreme to the other since getting here." Hunter frowned at his brother. "But, do me a favor and keep the touching to a minimum. She doesn't need you pawing her every time her emotions go crazy."

Sloan faked an indignant choke. "Pawing her?" He laughed softly. "Man, you've got it bad, and you don't even know it. Admit it, bro. You're attracted to her and feel more than a little possessive.

Damn. I thought I'd be the first one to fall. I'm the younger one." He laughed again at Hunter's low growl. "Okay. Don't punch me." He raised his hand and placed his other one over his heart. In a deep solemn voice he declared, "I swear not to paw Briana every time it's necessary."

Hunter gave him a hard stare. "Let's talk about that necessary part."

Before Sloan could reply, a slight noise was heard from where the two women were sleeping. Hunter stood in one smooth lunge. "It's Briana. She's been fretting in her sleep for awhile now."

"I'm surprised she fell asleep in the first place."

Hunter nodded. "She was exhausted after casting that Spell. And that's something we've got to be aware of, Sloan. The debilitating exhaustion after heavy spell casting may be a problem, later. We'll have to make sure to stay close when either of them use their magic in a big way." If they found themselves in a battle against sorcery, he didn't want to have to worry about making sure Briana was protected. He'd stay close at all times.

He walked over to where Briana lay sleeping. The blanket she'd had earlier was thrown to the side and she was tossing and turning. She looked fragile and small lying there, and some of the anger sitting deep inside him surge back to the surface. Sloan was right. He already felt more than a little possessive of her. But dammit, she was the reason they were here in this situation to begin with. She'd brought this into their lives, without giving them a choice.

She cried out softly, her face scrunching in a quick flash of fear. Hunter knelt down beside her and gently touched her shoulder. "Briana, wake up."

She came awake instantly, another cry escaping her. She lunged forward and locked her arms around his neck. Hunter lost his balance and fell down beside her. He rolled to his back and pulled her closer. She lay half over his upper body and hid her face against his neck. He jerked when he felt her hot tears on his skin.

"I'm so sorry," she whispered the words against his neck. "I never meant to involve you in this, Hunter. I wish I could send you back right now, but I can't. I don't know what to do. And I hate feeling this helpless."

"You're far from being helpless, sweetheart," he said. "I'm just glad you're on my side."

She sniffed. "You're just saying that so I'll stay calm. I can't, Hunter. I'm full of panicking thoughts."

"Just don't say any spells right now," he drawled, "and we'll both be happy."

"Ha ha." She lifted her head and stared down into his eyes.

He saw her fear, her uncertainty, her fragileness, shining in the dark green depths. A flare of protectiveness hit him hard. But he also saw strength and determination. And that made him proud without fully understanding why. He curled his hand around her neck, under her hair, and pressed her face back down. He shifted so that they were settled more comfortably.

"Go back to sleep," he murmured against her bent head. "We'll figure all this out tomorrow."

They had to. Too many people were depending on them now.

They were about to go into a battle against a Being—who, just yesterday he didn't believe even existed—and what the outcome of that war would be was anyone's guess.

But fighting against evil—in any form—was what he did best. The surge of anticipation startled him for a moment.

Then, he relished it.

✳

The castle sat atop a high hill. It looked like some fairy tale castle Briana had seen in books. Imposing and magical, at least three floors high, it glistened as though the brick construction was coated in a light film of glitter. A spiraling turret sat at each corner. Each floor had countless windows, tall and narrow, and covered in stained glass. The double, heavy oak front doors were at least ten feet wide and as tall.

They had passed through a smallish village—although it didn't resemble the way Briana thought villages were supposed to have looked like—and then climbed the smooth, well-tended path up the hill. All around them, on the hill and below, were countless flowers and greenery. Exotic, tropical flowers mixed with the vibrant shades of Scottish heather everywhere. Kassidy had explained that parallel worlds had some of the same things their sister world did. Thus the reason for the tropical flowers and greenery very much like those found in the real Florida.

Briana cringed every time Kassidy mentioned home. She wasn't sure if Hunter and Sloan were still mad at her for getting them in this weird predicament. Granted, Hunter had held her through the rest of the night, chasing away the nightmares every time one hit, and assuring her that all would be okay. He'd been so gentle. If she hadn't been upset she might have been able to enjoy being held so close to his hard body, feeling his hands rubbing her back and caressing her neck.

But when the morning came he had released her without saying anything. He and Sloan had abruptly turned into their counterpart detective personas. They kept Kassidy busy answering countless questions. Despite their no-nonsense attitude and nonstop interrogating, Kassidy took it all in stride as she led them through the village and up the hill to the castle. Briana liked the young woman. She seemed to be the proverbial calm eye of the storm, nothing ruffling her, and answering the firing questions as though she'd done it every day of her life. Yet, Briana had no doubt the red head would have a daunting temper if pushed the wrong way. There was a particular strength about her that Briana envied. Her spell casting was instantaneous and powerful. *Not like mine.*

Briana glanced at Hunter as he listened close to something Kassidy was explaining. Was that admiration in his dark gaze? She looked at Sloan. Yep. Both men were very impressed with Kassidy, no doubt about it. *Let's face it. They see me as a bumbling witch who can't control her powers. They're probably relieved that Kassidy is so level-headed and strong.*

She grimaced at her thoughts. In truth, she was very thankful that Kassidy was like that, too. She had no idea what part she was going to play in the coming days events but at least Hunter and Sloan would have one powerful witch on their side.

She just needed to get the Sphere, help Kassidy seal that door, and then find the right spell to get them home. *I can do this. No problem.*

Problem at twelve-o'clock. Briana stared in shock, choking back a small cry. Directly ahead of them two of last night's monsters stepped from the shrubbery and onto the path. Hunter and Sloan immediately jumped in front of the women, their bodies stiffening into a fighting stance. Beside her, Briana heard Kassidy mutter, "This can't be. It's daylight."

One of the men-monsters raised his hand as if to stop them from advancing. His body resembled a man's, but his face, arms, and hands had morphed into that of a bear. If that sight wasn't way-out-of-this-world-odd enough, hearing a human voice come out of his bear mouth was just as shocking.

"Need ... your ... help." The words were guttural, slurred together, tinged with a slight growling noise. "Will ... not ... hurt ... you."

"We're not promising the same," Hunter stated, his tone dangerous. "What do you want?"

"Help ... to ... die."

"That should be easy enough to do," Sloan said.

"Step aside, smart-mouthed knight," Kassidy stated as she pushed Sloan out of her way. He shot her a look mixed with disbelief and anger. "I can handle this."

"No ... you ... cannot ... She ... can."

Hunter took a step closer to Briana when the demon shifter pointed at her. "Come near her and I'll make sure you die," he warned.

"Only ... she ... can ... help."

"Why?" Kassidy frowned in confusion. "I've tried everything I can think of to destroy you and nothing has worked. What can she do that I can't?"

"Change ... us ... back."

Briana shook her head. If Kassidy hadn't been able to change them then she knew she couldn't either. "I don't understand."

"Your ... power ... is ... otherworld."

Granted, she and Kassidy weren't the same with their powers, but she didn't think that hers being different because of where she came from would make a difference here now. Not in this situation. She'd never tried shapeshifting spells before. "I threatened a peacock once," she told them, "but I never followed through with changing him." She shook her head again. "I don't think I can help you."

"You ... will ... not ... try?"

Briana heard the vulnerability and distress in the growling words and it touched her deeply. She clamped down on the rising uncertainty that wanted to control her. What if she could do something? If she could change the monsters back to men, would that take away the sorcerer's only army? No matter what the outcome would be, she knew she couldn't live with herself if she didn't at least try.

"I can try," she told them. "I will need a few things before I cast the spell."

Kassidy nodded. "I have everything you might need, in the Castle."

"Forget it, Briana," Hunter told her as he turned to look at her. "We have no way of knowing if this is a trick or not. I'm not letting these beasts anywhere close to you." He frowned darkly at her. "And besides, if your spell backfired, we might end up with something worse than this."

Briana felt her face flush with anger from his words. "Thanks for the vote of confidence," she muttered. "But the last time I checked, Hunter, you had no say over what I do. And besides," she mimicked his words, "Sloan can always be there with me and—hold me if I need to be calm."

"Little witch." Hunter glared at her, an odd glint in the dark blue-grey of his eyes.

Briana's heart stuttered. He looked like he was ready to throw her across his lap and spank her. A thrill of lust shot through her at the thought. Wrong place, wrong time. Yet, she couldn't help but wonder if there ever would be the right time for them ...

"I don't know what you do in your world," Kassidy interrupted the tense moment. "But here, we act fast. If you're willing to try, Briana, then we must do it now. If there's a chance you can shift them back to human men, then we've just found a valuable weapon we weren't expecting." She turned to Sloan. "Come with me inside, and we'll get the tools she will need." Glancing at Briana and then back at Hunter, she asked, "Will you do the spell sky-clad?"

Briana couldn't break free from Hunter's stormy gaze. She nodded her head. "It will probably work best that way."

"What is sky-clad?" Hunter's frown turned darker.

There was no way around it and she blushed when she answered as casually as she could manage, "Naked."

Hunter opened his mouth and then shut it. His eyes darkened to blue-black and his stare turned intense and hard. Briana's heart raced at the look on his face. Finally he seemed to get control of his anger and turned away from her. He strode past Sloan. "Stay with her," he muttered in a near growl, "Keep her calm. And kill either of these beasts if they take even one step toward her."

He grabbed Kassidy by her elbow and stomped up the remaining distance to the castle doors. If his body language was any indication, Briana was sure he was a man riding the edge. Unfortunately, she was the cause.

Sloan touched her arm and she immediately felt a calm slide over her body. Thank the Goddess for small favors. He looked at the two men-monsters. "That was my brother's way of telling you that even if I don't have a weapon, I'll rip the two of you to shreds if you try to harm her. So, do yourselves a favor and don't move."

Neither demon shifter answered his challenge, and Briana sighed out in relief. She didn't doubt Sloan would be able to protect her, but she didn't want to find out what it would take to defeat demons like this. She wasn't sure Sloan would come out of the fight alive either ...

A few tense-filled minutes later Kassidy and Hunter returned. Kassidy motioned for them to follow her off the path and into a cluster of trees. Tall imposing oak sat side by side with Beech trees, circling a small oval clearing. A thin river-stream ran through the circle, its water gurgling loudly as it flowed.

"To witches, rivers are the source of Life," Kassidy explained to Hunter and Sloan. "And our forest groves are considered especially hallowed. Oak and beech can also represent the Tree of Life—like the sacred willow."

Briana watched as she carefully emptied the contents of the bag she was holding onto the ground. White candles, a yarrow plant, rosemary and sage, all things that represented protection. Hunter placed a small copper cauldron next to the items. Briana could see that it was already filled with some kind of liquid. It looked like melted silver, thick, with a touch of glimmer. Was that what she thought it might be? Kassidy confirmed with a nod, "Yes, it is the Sacred Elixir. I have had it for many centuries. It will strengthen your spell."

Despite the seriousness of the situation, Sloan choked out a shocked, "Centuries?" He stared at Kassidy with just a little bit of fear in his eyes. "Just how old are you, witch?"

"So not the time, Sloan," Briana murmured. She hid her grin. But the humor of the moment was lost as soon as he and Hunter turned to stare at her, their brows raised in question. She gasped, indignant. "I am not old! Don't forget that time here passes different than in our world. Kassidy's centuries could probably be compared to decades in our time."

"Yes," Kassidy murmured with a definitely wicked smile. "That's right."

"I don't believe her." Sloan glared at Kassidy. Hunter, on the other hand, was staring at her so intently it took every ounce of willpower she had not to squirm. Instead, she muttered one more time with a little more force, "I am not old."

A gruff, cough-growl broke into the moment. The two demon shifters stood side by side, watching them with oddly gleaming eyes. Briana suddenly felt apprehension snake through her. What if Hunter was right and this was some kind of trick? What if they wanted her to spell cast for some specific reason? There was every possibility that she could do more damage than good.

Could she risk it?

Her fear of the unknown consequences was suddenly reaffirmed when one of the demon shifters growled out, his words a clear warning,

"Do ... the ... spell ... witch ... you ... must."

Chapter Fifteen

Briana shot a surprised look at Hunter when he growled right back at the demons, the sound even nastier than theirs. A thrill of feminine delight raced through her. He was so protective.

"Why is it so important to do the spell ... now?" Hunter demanded.

The demon shifters didn't answer. Their animalistic expressions remained blank. The sickening apprehension in her stomach increased and Briana mentally chanted a calming mantra. Something wasn't exactly right here, but she couldn't pin it down. She glanced at Kassidy and noticed her worried frown too. Hunter and Sloan's protective stances became more aggressive as they stepped in front of her and Kassidy. The tension radiating off the demon shifters was so strong, it felt like a buffeting wave of belligerent animosity.

"Kassidy, do you have the power to transport?" Hunter asked low, glancing at her over his shoulder.

Briana started to say, "I do." but thought better of it. Right now wasn't the time to risk a spell going awry. She grimaced. With her luck, Hunter would have his hand over her mouth before she could utter the first word. One of these days she was going to have to really confront him about his attitude.

Kassidy stepped next to Briana and suddenly waved her hands, at the same time uttering foreign sounding words. In the poof of a split second Briana blinked and found her self in the middle of a huge hall inside the castle. "This is beautiful," she murmured, looking around. The floors were shiny marble, the walls glistening-glitter brick, and the few odd pieces of furniture were all solid oak. It was luxurious yet all too surreal in one package.

Beside her Hunter leaned in close and teasingly whispered, "At least when she transports, someone doesn't end up naked."

She couldn't help it. She winked at him. "What's the fun in that?"

Hunter's lips landed close to her ear, his breath warm. "I didn't say I preferred her way."

"Will you two stop?" Sloan groaned dramatically. "Or get a room." He looked around the huge hall. "I'm assuming this place has rooms. And what the hell was that transporting deal? Someone could have warned me. I nearly swallowed my tongue, dammit."

Kassidy raised her brows in silent mockery at him and he glared back. Briana figured now was the time to change the subject. She looked at Hunter. "Why did you ask Kassidy to transport us out of there? I could have performed the spell."

Hunter frowned at her. "Something wasn't right."

"Yeah," Sloan agreed. "The aggression coming off those two beasts was growing by the second. What do you think they were up to, Hunter?"

Hunter ran a hand over his jaw. "They said it was because they wanted help. But they were too concentrated on Briana for my comfort. Did you notice that no matter who else talked, they never took their eyes off her? Even though they acknowledged Kassidy's comment about trying to change them back, they never stopped staring at Briana."

"Maybe it was because they recognized I was a witch, and wondered if I had any other powers that Kassidy might not have." At least, she hoped that was the answer. Anything else was just plain freaky. *Eeew.* The last thing she needed or wanted was monsters fascinated with her.

Kassidy sighed. "It's more likely the sorcerer who controls them has discovered that you are here. He knows I borrowed the Sphere to stop his plans. He is highly intelligent and would guess that the Sphere's guardian would come for it." She turned away and started across the wide hall with determined strides. "Time is running out. Come with me, Briana, and I will take you to the Sphere."

Briana hurried after her, elated at knowing that she would finally have the Sphere back in her possession. She was confident that once she had it back, they would be able to stop the sorcerer and permanently close that hell door. She wasn't ready to accept any other alternatives ...

Kassidy led them up three sets of stairs and then up another spiral staircase that led straight to the highest turret room. Along the way, they saw at least ten bedrooms on each floor, all luxuriously decorated as though they were straight out of a fashion magazine that specialized in castle décor-with-a-touch-of-fairytale. It was beyond surreal and Briana couldn't help but be a little awed by the otherworldly grandeur. If the situation hadn't been so dire, she would have loved to explore the place more. But there were priorities right now. Feeling anxious to get to the Sphere, she ran into Kassidy.

Kassidy stopped in front of a steel door and waved her hand over the lock. It clicked open with a loud snap that echoed back into the hall behind them. There was only one piece of furniture in the small circular room. Right in the center of the room sat a high, three-legged pedestal encircled by a glowing flame of light. On the seat of the pedestal sat the Sphere.

Briana gasped and rushed forward. Kassidy shouted in warning, "Wait! The protection spell will hurt you." Briana skidded to a halt inches from the surrounding aura and shot Kassidy an impatient glare. "Hurry, Kass. I need to have it in my hands. Now."

The urgency nearly overwhelmed her. Because the moment she had stepped into the room she saw the very thing she had been fearfully dreading all along. The live Willow Tree inside the Sphere was wilting.

Dying.

Oh, Goddess. This can't be happening. As soon as Kassidy broke the protection spell Briana reached out and grasped the Sphere in her trembling hands. She was shaking so much she thought she might fall so she held the Sphere tighter, her breath coming in agitated pants. "It can't be too late," she murmured, fear making her voice hoarse. "Damn it, Kassidy! If you knew about the Sphere then, you also knew what would happen if it wasn't in my possession. What have you done?"

Hunter came over to stand next to her. He touched her arm. "What's wrong, Briana? You have the Sphere; isn't that the important thing?"

Briana blinked away tears, her heart thudding in fear. "It's dying, Hunter. The Sphere can't be away from me very long or the tree will die. I don't know if I can repair the damage already done. I don't know if I have that kind of power!" She'd never experienced such a profound feeling of helplessness, and hated feeling it now.

"Calm down, honey," Sloan said soothingly. "Try it anyway. You can do it if you stay calm."

Briana shook her head. They didn't really understand the severity of the situation. The living Willow had been blessed and enchanted by her ancestors, witches that were more powerful than any other yet to walk the world. The only power she had on the Sphere was her ancestral connection.

"I won't apologize for taking it," Kassidy stated, her tone firm. "It's needed here to close that door."

Hunter scowled at her. "A lot of good it's doing you now."

"I need space," Briana finally muttered, "Complete quiet. Empty the room." She would try, but Goddess only knew if she had the power it would take. She inhaled a deep calming breath and then exhaled slowly, willing her heart to slow its racing beat. There was no other choice. She had to heal the Tree. Nothing else was acceptable.

Sloan hesitated at the door before leaving. "Calm enough, Bri?"

"Yes." *As calm as I can be knowing the world is depending on my skills.*

"We'll be right outside the door," Hunter told her, touching her cheek with a fleeting caress. He caught her gaze with his and her heart stuttered with the penetrating look shining in the dark blue-grey depths. There was concern there, as well as confidence. It was that assuring confidence she'd never thought to see him have with her that now gave her the strength she needed. He smiled at her before turning away and leaving with Sloan and Kassidy.

Alone now, Briana set the Sphere back on the pedestal. "Goddess," she whispered, "Help me now, in this most needed moment of time. Hear me. Strengthen me so that I may be able to strengthen the Tree." She stepped into the very center of the room and raised both hands toward the ceiling. "I call upon my ancestors, the creators of the Sphere. Hear me from across time and space. Empower me with the sacred knowledge and the magical strength I need to heal the Tree."

Nothing happened at first. Ominous silence echoed in the room.

Briana willed her emotions to remain calm. *Hear me!* She mentally pleaded, heart beating way too fast with her chaotic doubts. But ... what if they didn't hear her? What if being in a parallel world prevented the Powers-that-Be from reaching her? What would she do then? Taking the Sphere back to her world—that is, once she figured out how to get them back—wouldn't solve anything. If she took the Sphere from Kassidy's world without sealing that door, then hell would be released. No. She couldn't chance it. She had to heal the Sphere here, first.

She lowered her hands and placed them on the Sphere. A sudden arcing surge of power shot from the glass dome and straight into her hands and up her arms. It was exhilarating. But ... only for that one, long, hope-filled moment.

Then suddenly, the power shooting through her abruptly reversed its direction and unerringly arced back to the Sphere. Taking with it every ounce of energy she had. She barely managed to call out Hunter's name before the horrifying blackness swamped her and she felt herself falling. Then ... nothing.

✳

Her first conscious thoughts were a little confused. Warmth surrounded her. Strong arms. A hard body touching hers, skin to skin. Bare skin. Okay, that forced her eyes open. She lifted her heavy lids and stared straight up into Hunter's eyes.

"What happened?" Her voice came out sounding hoarse, as though she had been shouting for a long time. She tried to force her scattered thoughts to settle so that she could concentrate on her last memory. But her mind didn't really want to dwell on sane thoughts right then. No, it wanted to focus on Hunter's bare body pressed so tight to her bare one. "Why are we naked?"

His smile was wicked, sending her heartbeat into overdrive. He shifted, hugging her closer and then settling back against a pile of large pillows. "You didn't think I would let Sloan hold you, did you? He may be your calm-in-the-eye-of-the-storm, but hell, I'm the only one allowed to see you naked."

The possessive growl in his tone caused a shiver to streak through her. "Okay," she said, hiding her smile. "I understand that, but why are we both naked at this particular moment?"

"Body heat," he explained casually despite the sensual hum in his voice. "You were cold as ice and I figured it was the fastest way to warm you. I thought about sitting by the fireplace but then realized the bed would be more comfortable."

"You are deliberately trying to confuse me," she accused. Why did she have the bad feeling he was holding something back? She tried to sit up but his arms were holding her too tight. "What really happened?" Sudden panic hit as soon as she asked the question and she instantly remembered the Sphere. "Goddess! What happened to the Sphere? Where is it? Hunter, let me go. I need to get to it."

"Stop, Briana," he warned the same time he tightened his arms. "You're not going anywhere until I'm sure you're okay. Not only was your body frozen, you barely had a pulse. I don't know what the hell happened in that room but we'll figure it out before I let you go back in there."

"Don't you dare treat me condescendingly like that," she told him, angry yet horrified at what his words really meant. *What happened?* "You have no say in what I do or don't do. Now, let me go."

Hunter suddenly moved, rolling her in his arms and effortlessly maneuvering her body underneath him in mere seconds. He leaned heavily onto her, staring down at her with an expression of anger and something more. "Damn it. I can't keep doing this, Briana. You're driving me crazy with your recklessness. Every time I think I've got you safe, you prove me wrong. I have this constant fear that you'll do something to endanger your life and no power on earth will keep you safe. And that's a pretty bad state to be in, considering I haven't known you long. I don't want to feel this way, sweetheart, but until I can feel like I'm in control of this weird situation we're in, you're just going to have to put up with me being overbearing."

"Protective."

Hunter blinked rapidly twice and asked, "Huh?"

Briana smiled. She wanted to kiss him. "It's not so much that you're overbearing—it's that you are protective. I like that. A lot. You're my 'knight in shining armor'—even if you don't want to be." Oh how she wished he wanted to be.

Hunter shifted slightly and Briana gasped. His hard, hot erection was pressing in just the right spot between her thighs. He grinned devilishly. "Knight, huh? Could be worse. You could have picked Sloan for the job."

"Could have." She couldn't help it, she was enjoying this intimate moment more than she wanted to admit, and she smiled teasingly. "After all, he's the one with the power to keep me calm. Maybe I should think about that."

"I love my brother," he stated in a deadly serious tone, "but if he keeps touching you I'm going to beat the hell out of him." He gave her a hard stare. "Think on that, baby."

She loved that possessive growl in his tone. If only they had the luxury of time to pursue the growing feelings between them ...

"Hunter," she sighed his name. She closed her eyes tight for a long moment and tried to concentrate on what was important rather than the delicious, hot, hardness pressing onto her. "I need to know what happened with the Sphere."

He frowned, shaking his head. He rolled to his side and pulled her close again. "I don't know. We heard this loud roaring sound and then I heard you call my name. When I got to you, you were unconscious and cold. Scared the hell out of me. Kassidy put another protection spell around the Sphere and I carried you out of there. What is the last thing you remember?"

She focused determinedly, pulling up the memory of the last few minutes with the Sphere. "I had touched the Sphere and then felt this incredible surge of power radiate from it into my body. But then, I suddenly felt as though all my energy was being drained. I remember falling. That's it." It wasn't enough. She needed to know what had happened.

She abruptly sat up. The blanket Hunter had wrapped over them fell, exposing her bare breasts. She gasped and hastily clutched it, holding it against her chest. She glared down at him, her breath catchy. His handsome features instantly darkened with obvious desire and his eyes suddenly glowed with heat. "Get that look off your face," she choked out, nerves tingling in reaction. "Right now there are more important things to think about."

Hunter reached up and placed his hands over hers where she held the blanket. His words were husky, low, firm. "The Sphere is safely spell-protected. The tower room is securely locked. There is nothing you can do until morning. The castle is settled in for the night. Sloan has finally gone to bed in his own room. Kassidy has assured me that the entire place is impenetrable." He slowly tugged her down, bringing her inch by slow inch closer. He growled huskily, "There is nothing more important right now ... than this."

He lifted his head to meet her descending one. His mouth captured her whisper of his name and he immediately shoved his tongue past her lips. The open mouth kiss was hot and devouring. Briana lost her breath, and then moaned in acceptance as she let him pull her down the rest of the way.

Chapter Sixteen

Her body melted against his, every bare inch feeling scorched by his heat. Hunter wrapped one hand around her nape beneath her hair. His other hand moved from her neck to rest between her shoulder blades for a caressing moment before slowly inching down her back. The blanket slipped away from their bodies and he finished pushing it aside when his hand reached the indent in her lower back. His kiss turned hotter, his tongue moving in and out of her mouth in a tantalizingly slow, erotic rhythm. She moaned again and kissed him back, mimicking his movements. Hard shivers of desire raced through her until her whole body was shaking in anticipation.

One sliding caress had his hand down and over one butt cheek. He lightly squeezed the globe, and then smoothed his hand over to the other one. He groaned into her mouth and deepened his kiss. Briana couldn't stop the squirm and she made a little mewling sound as she moved her hips in rhythm with his clenching hand on her soft flesh. Beneath her, his shaft was hot and hard and pushing up insistently. One little move in the right direction and he would be inside her.

Hunter grasped her hips and suddenly turned her to lie beneath him. Briana gasped in a much needed inhale of air as his lips left hers and traveled in a hot path across her cheek to her ear. His hands gripped her hips, holding her still.

"Slow, baby," he murmured against her ear. "I've been waiting for this since the first time I saw you naked. I'm not going to let anything rush us."

She smiled knowingly. "I don't think our bodies are going to allow us to go slow."

His erection was already pushing against her center, seeking entrance, and he groaned loud and hard. "I want to be inside you so bad, it's killing me to hold back. But I want to savor this. I want to kiss you more—you have the sweetest lips. I want—hell. Stop moving like that, Briana."

Somehow he managed to lift his body slightly, pulling away from her aching center. He stared down into her eyes for a long poignant moment and then lowered his head to capture her lips again. This time the kiss was slow, thorough, filled with restrained passion. After a few minutes he kissed his way over her chin and then down to her neck.

"Your skin is so soft. From the first moment I saw you I've had this constant itch to touch you. Caress you. Kiss every inch of you."

He kissed across her throat and then briefly kissed each shoulder. Then, slowly, his hot mouth moved down her collarbone and to her breast. Briana arched with a small cry of delight the moment his lips touched her there. She whispered his name, encouraging him. She felt his smile against the sensitive skin of her breast right before his lips opened and he sucked her nipple deep into his mouth. Her moan and his groan simultaneously blended.

Hunter pulled her nipple deep into his mouth and swirled his tongue around the distended point. He suddenly released it and moved to the opposite one. "Mmm. Sweet as berries," he murmured huskily. "I could become addicted to this."

Briana squirmed and moaned, her body restless and on fire. His slow, sensuous torture was killing her. She wanted to ask him to stop—just long enough to catch her breath. Ha. Instead, she begged him not to. "That feels so good," she managed to get out. "Please, don't stop."

She groaned out a protest when he did just that. But then, she couldn't manage to make another sound as he lowered his head and trailed his lips down her stomach to her navel. His grip on her hips tightened in warning right before he kissed lower, his mouth sliding over the top of her bare mound in one long hot caress.

"Hunter," she choked out.

"Shh. Don't move. Just a few more kisses." He groaned, the sound hoarse. "Just one taste, first."

It was the only warning she got. His mouth opened over her

feminine lips, and his tongue slipped out for a long sweep. If he hadn't been holding her hips down, she would have arched right off the bed with the incredible feel from his mouth and tongue now devouring her there. His tongue pushed deep into her, licking and stroking. She cried out from the overwhelming sensations, felt the impending orgasm threaten as it hovered just out of reach. She dug her hands into his hair, pressed his head harder against her. He responded by suddenly slipping a finger deep into her and unerringly touching her most oversensitive places. Stars burst behind her eyelids and she rode the exhilarating wave with a soft cry that was full of stark and vivid emotion.

Minutes later her breathing calmed, and she opened her eyes to see Hunter with his chin resting on her stomach right above her mound staring at her with a look so hot she lost her breath all over again.

"Again," he growled out in a husky low timbre. "I want to taste you more."

He started to lower his head when the loud crash startled them both. Hunter sat up immediately, his body shielding hers. Another crash sounded.

"What is it? Where is it coming from?"

"Damned if I know." Hunter jumped off the bed and grabbed his pants from the floor. He pulled them on and then sat back down on the bed to quickly put his boots on. "Kassidy said the castle was impenetrable with her protection spell. Stay here, while I go check."

"No way." She rolled to the side of the bed and leaned down to grab her dress. "Now isn't the time to play macho and try to protect me, Hunter."

"Will it ever be?"

Briana stopped in the motion of slipping on her shoes. His muttered words were barely audible but she'd clearly heard the unspoken question behind the words. This sudden tension between them so soon after that intimate time earlier was more than a little disconcerting. "Hunter, I didn't mean to sound like a feminist. It's just that I can't wait in the background while everyone else fights my battles for me. If there's something I can do, then I need to be there to help."

Hunter put his shirt on and headed for the bedroom door.

Without looking back at her he quietly said, "I know, Briana. I just have to figure out how to deal with it."

Briana hurried out into the long hall after him. Two doors down, Sloan came rushing out of his room. He and Hunter met up going down the stairs. She raced to keep up with their long strides.

"It sounded like it came directly from somewhere below," Sloan said. "But the only thing beneath this floor is the basement, according to Kassidy, and it's supposed to be closed off."

Briana tried to keep the fear out of her voice but failed. "Kassidy said the basement is where the hell door is located."

Hunter and Sloan sprinted off in a fast run down the remaining stairs. They met Kassidy hurrying across the wide hall. She stopped long enough for them to glimpse the fear on her face. Her gaze flew to Briana. "Hurry, Briana. We may not have the Sphere to help but we have to do whatever we can to secure that door."

They ran, their fear increasing when another loud crash sounded. Kassidy shouted the opening spell on the locked doors before they even reached them. The wide oak panels swung open and they rushed in.

Huge, cave-like, the round circular basement was made of pure steel walls and steel floor. Completely empty.

"Empty?" Briana stumbled in her haste to stop before crashing into Kassidy. "Where did that sound come from?"

Kassidy moved slowly to the center of the room. "From the other side of the door."

"And the door is where, exactly?" Sloan demanded.

She stopped in the center and made a circle with her hands as she turned around. "Here. The basement is the door."

"Start explaining," Hunter growled out as another loud crash boomed and then echoed around the huge cavern.

Kassidy continued drawing her invisible circle with her hands and turning around, murmuring words under her breath. Briana moved to stand next to her. "The hell door is in a parallel world too," she explained to Hunter and Sloan. "It's not visible until—until it's actually opened."

"I hate sounding stupid," Sloan stated, sarcasm tinging his tone, "But how the hell do you know it's there if you can't see it, and how do you plan on sealing it?"

"The Sphere has the power to seal it," Briana told them. She cringed. "But not if the Tree is dying. It needs to be at full strength. Then, I would cast a sealing spell that would effectively block any entrance into this world or any other."

"For now, we will have to use what powers we have, combined, and put up a block strong enough to hold until the Tree is healed." Kassidy pointed to a spot a few yards to her right. "There is the main opening. Stand over the rune symbol you see on the floor, Briana."

Briana didn't hesitate and moved into position. Yards away from her Hunter and Sloan watched her with intent gazes. Hunter's lids were lowered, shielding his thoughts from her. But she could feel the tension radiating off of him.

"Is this dangerous?" Hunter asked Kassidy although he kept his gaze locked with Briana's. "Is Briana going to be safe doing this?" Kassidy didn't answer for a long moment. Sloan actually growled at her. "Damn it, woman. Answer him."

She turned her back on him. "If we fail and the door opens even the slightest, something might come through. Briana will be the first hit. But she has to stand over the rune because it is her ancestral connection to the Sphere that gives her the power to block the door."

Briana saw Hunter's jaw clench and his face flush with anger. But he didn't say anything. He simply moved closer to her until he was less than a yard away. He snared her gaze, and his voice was low and deep. "If anything does come through, baby, I swear I'll get it before it reaches you. Just do what you have to do and know I'll keep you safe."

Briana felt hot tears flooding her eyes and blinked hard to clear them. "I know." And she did. Hunter would do anything in his power to protect her.

Sloan came to stand next to Hunter. "Are you calm enough, honey?"

She was. Oddly enough, the fear of what might happen if they didn't block the door wasn't overriding her strength and determination. She nodded. "Thanks, Sloan."

"Just as well," Hunter muttered low. "If I have to see you touch her one more time, I'm going to kick your ass, brother."

"Yeah, right. Get used to it, bro."

"Excuse me," Kassidy's voice was harsh and sarcastic. "Priorities here."

Sloan sent her a grin part devilish, part sensual. "You're just jealous," he told her with another smirk. "But hey, sweetheart, I'll be glad to come over there and hold you if you think you need me to."

Kassidy shot him a glare nasty enough to singe him if he'd been close enough. "I have no idea what you're talking about, or why your brother would even allow you to touch his woman, but now isn't the time for your antics. So, shut up." She turned to Briana. "Ready?"

Briana bit back her laugh at Sloan's stunned expression. She immediately sobered when a low, deep rumble shook the floor beneath them. "Let's do this."

She and Kassidy took in deep inhales and then slowly exhaled. Then they chanted the mantra to open their Chakras. Minutes later they began to simultaneously chant the words to the sealing spell. Their voices were strong, their words powerful. Almost immediately a whoosh of wind spun through the huge room, gaining in speed as it neared them. It buffeted against the two women but oddly never touched the men. Hunter started to reach out and grabbed Briana when the wind pushed her back a step but she shook her head. "Touching me will break the circle."

The driving force of the wind became stronger and both women were hard pressed to remain standing. They strengthened the chanting, raising their voices in an attempt to be heard over the roaring wind.

Suddenly the wind's perimeter narrowed down to swirling around only Briana. A few feet away Kassidy collapsed to the floor. Hunter shouted at Sloan to get to the fallen woman. He braced his feet apart and stiffened his body, preparing to grab Briana. She saw the stark look of determination on his face, saw his fear for her, but she couldn't say anything. The wind was so strong she could barely breathe. Goddess, help her, but something was seriously wrong. The wind should have been helping her instead of fighting against her. She wanted to cry out to Hunter to break the circle but she couldn't. Suddenly she started spinning in the ferocious force of wind. And she knew. *Knew* the dark power from beyond the door was trying to pull her through.

She opened her mouth to try and scream to Hunter for help. But she didn't need to. He lunged forward and grabbed her, wrapping his arms tight around her. His momentum was so rough it shoved them out of the velocity of wind and took them both to the floor in a hard, bone-bruising roll. Hunter somehow managed to make sure his body took the brunt of the fall and the roll as he kept Briana securely wrapped in his arms and on top of him. What breath she had left whooshed out of her on a broken scream as they skidded at least four or five yards across the hard, cold, steel floor.

Stunned, they lay there and tried to catch their breath. Unable to get enough energy to even raise her head off Hunter's chest, Briana took in deep gulps of air and clung to him. He'd saved her life. If he hadn't been stubborn enough to ignore her warning about breaking the circle ... She didn't even want to think about what might have happened. A hard shiver shook her from head to toes. Hunter tightened his arms and whispered hoarsely, "It's alright, baby. I have you now."

And if she had a choice she would stay right there. Safe in his strong arms. But she couldn't. Something had gone dangerously wrong and they needed to figure it out as quickly as possible. She raised her head and looked down into his face. Their gazes locked. She saw herself reflected back in the dark, swirling blue-grey depths filled with heat. And ... looking deeper she saw something more. This time when she trembled it wasn't an aftereffect of the fear. He could do that to her. With just one searing, hot look. No matter the circumstances.

"Hunter," Sloan shouted from across the room. "Are you two okay?"

Hunter slowly sat up, careful to keep Briana secure in his arms. "Yeah. I think so." His gaze was thorough as it roamed over her. "Hurt anywhere, sweetheart?"

She shook her head. She was sure she'd have a few bruises later, and her chest was still tight with lingering fear, but otherwise she was fine.

"Then get the hell over here fast," Sloan called out. "Kassidy is in bad shape."

They got to their feet and hurried over to where Sloan was kneeling by a very-still Kassidy. Briana came down on her knees beside her. She choked back a gasp. The woman's face was deathly white, and a small amount of blood trickled out of the corner of her mouth.

"Kassidy! What is it? What happened?"

Kassidy cleared her throat twice before she could manage to talk. Her voice came out sounding weak and hoarse. "He's more powerful than I thought." She grabbed Briana's hand. "If he can control the perimeter of the hell door, it means he has somehow managed to get inside. Here."

"He can't be inside the castle." Briana had felt the power of the protection spell Kassidy had used. It was incredibly strong, unbreakable. The witch had powers even Briana had never encountered.

"Not physically," Kassidy answered, her voice breaking. "But he is powerful enough to extend his range of sorcery into my domain. No evil has ever broke past my barriers. Ever." Tears slipped from her eyes and rolled down her cheeks. "We can't fight him and win, Briana. Maybe not even with the Sphere. If he is that powerful, nothing we do will stop him from opening that door."

Chapter Seventeen

"If witchcraft can't stop the son of a—" Hunter grated out harshly, "Then I can. Like hell I'm going to sit back and let him win."

He might be temporarily stuck in a parallel world, but he was still the same man he was days ago. And that man never accepted defeat when it came to fighting the bad guy. The bastard had overstepped his boundaries when he'd tried to hurt Briana.

Sloan nodded his head. "Yeah. Maybe we need a change of tactics. Instead of fighting magic with magic, we can use plain ole human power."

"No." Kassidy's voice was weaker. Hunter saw Briana chew on her bottom lip, her lovely features marred with worry and fear. He touched her arm to get her attention, and then mouthed the words "Can you help her?"

She nodded her head. "We need to get Kassidy to her room. I'll do a healing spell."

Sloan carefully gathered the woman into his arms and stood up. "Let's get out of this hell hole," he muttered.

Kassidy slowly lifted her head off Sloan's shoulders. "Briana. You have to seal the locks on the door of the basement. It might make a small deterrent."

Hunter stayed with Briana while she spell cast the huge iron locks on the basement door and Sloan carried Kassidy upstairs. Despite all she'd just been through, her voice was calm as she cast the spell and her hands steady as she held them over the locks. Admiration and pride swelled in him. She was one amazing woman. She'd walked into that circle with confidence. And she'd bravely tried to hold out when things started getting out of control.

Damn. The soul-deep fear that hit him when she'd started

spinning had nearly brought him to his knees. He couldn't get to her fast enough. The moment he'd grabbed her, relief flooded him, even as they fell out of the whirlwind and were forcibly slung across the floor. Even now, despite feeling the fear waft off her, he could see that she was trying to take it minute by minute and figure out what to do next. She had an inner strength few women in her circumstances would have had. And even though it struck at his pride that she fought him on trying to protect her all the time, he had to admit her willful strength only added to her inner beauty. He suddenly grinned. She was tempered sanity and sweet craziness all mixed in one, and had somehow managed to turn his whole life upside down. One thing was certain. Life with her would never be dull.

Whoa. Don't go there. Now wasn't the time to be thinking about a relationship. Hell, they had to get out of this alive before they even thought about the days after.

Still, he couldn't deny that he was more than just attracted to her. He wanted her with a passion that surpassed anything he'd ever felt for any other woman. Even in the direst of moments his thoughts strayed to the need to touch her. Kiss her. Make love to her. He was man enough to admit his feelings for the intriguing woman were amazingly strong, and undeniably deep.

He placed his hand on her lower back as they walked back up the stairs. She glanced at him from under lowered lashes, and his heart skipped a beat. Even worried about someone or something, she still managed to look adorably vulnerable. "What is it?"

She was silent as they reached the first floor and then started up the stairs to the bedrooms. He didn't push. He knew both of them were still experiencing the adrenaline spurts from the incident in the basement.

Finally she took a deep breath and released it on a shaky sigh. "You saved my life."

He distinctively heard the vulnerability in her tone. "Yeah," he teased, "I guess that means you belong to me now. Isn't that what the old quote says?"

She smiled, making him grin back. "Something like that. It's just that—" She paused and chewed on her bottom lip for a moment before rushing on, "Earlier I made this whole deal about being able to take care of myself. Then, when things got out of control ... my first instinct was to reach for you."

He could have pushed, but instinctively knew now wasn't the time. Later, when they were alone again …

"Reach for me anytime, Briana," he said softly. "I'll be there." He realized the deeper implications of that vow, and knew she did too.

Sloan was standing by Kassidy's bedside when they got there. He frowned. "She lost consciousness a moment ago. But before she did she kept muttering something about men being stupid." His lips turned up in a slight smile. "The damn woman can't bear the thought of men doing her job."

Briana sat down on the bed next to Kassidy and touched her cheek. "Her skin is clammy and pale. I don't know what happened to her. The only thing I can come up with is that she must have been hit by a surge of power when that wind pushed her out of the circle." She placed both her hands on Kassidy's head and closed her eyes. She intoned ancient sounding, Celtic words, her voice soft and firm. Hunter moved closer to her. He wasn't taking any more chances. Every time either woman spell-spoke in a defensive, intrusive way, something happened in retaliation.

Briana's soft-spoken words continued for several minutes. Then, Kassidy suddenly gasped in a loud suck of air and opened her eyes. Hunter noticed the color return to her face immediately. He looked at Briana. For one frightening moment her face was deathly pale. With a shake of her head, her skin tone changed back to its peaches and cream color. He breathed out a sigh of relief.

Kassidy sat up. "Thank you," she said gratefully to Briana. But then she turned an angry stare on Hunter and Sloan. "Are you crazy? You can't think for one minute that humans can defeat someone as powerful as the sorcerer. That is simply suicidal."

Hunter silently acknowledged that the woman's reasoning had everything to do with the fact they were humans in a world not their own and she was the source of power here. But, dammit, her defense wasn't working. It was time to try something else.

He folded his arms over his chest. "Granted," he drawled, "It might be suicidal. But what other choice do we have here? You're an intelligent woman, Kassidy. I know you're starting to notice that every time you or Briana try to do a defense spell it backfires. Briana's presence in the tower room caused something to strike out at her. Your spell in the cellar nearly opened that damn door instead of closing it. It stands to reason this might happen every time either of you spell cast against anything this sorcerer has long range power over."

"We have to keep trying," Briana told him.

"Not the same way you're going about it now." His mind was quickly forming a battle strategy. If they could find out where this sorcerer was hiding ... "We need to fight back in a way that bastard sorcerer isn't expecting."

Sloan paced a few feet away, deep in thought. He snapped his fingers. "What if we get together an army?" He looked at Kassidy. "How many people around here? Are there other villages, a town, even a city? There has to be enough citizens who aren't willing to let Evil take over their lives."

Kassidy shook her head. "We are in a very remote area. That is why one of the doors is here. We're unknown and isolated completely. The people are direct descendents from those who originally built the castle over the door's location. If you count women and children, there are less than a hundred in the village."

Hunter didn't like the sound of that. Damn. Obviously an army was out of the question against such powerful evil. "How many rooms in this place?"

"Three floors, with fifteen bedrooms each. Too, there is the great hall, the kitchen area, the drawing room, library, four turret rooms, and the ... basement."

"I counted less than forty five houses in the village," Hunter noted aloud. "This shouldn't be a problem."

"What are you talking about?" Kassidy frowned at him. She looked at Briana then. "Have you been with this man long? Does he always try to take control like this?"

"Hey," Hunter growled, "He is right here. Damn woman, you're even more stubborn than Briana. This isn't 'taking control'. This is fighting with what we have, and planning to win. What part of winning this battle isn't sinking in?"

"It's getting late," Sloan interjected smoothly. "And those monsters come out at night. Do you think we have enough time, Hunter?"

Hunter nodded. "With Kassidy's cooperation."

Kassidy opened her mouth to say something and Hunter saw

Briana place her hand on her arm and shake her head. He held his grin back. His little witch may have a stubborn streak too, but at least she knew when to fight and when to back away for the time being.

"We'll help any way we can," Briana told him. Kassidy finally nodded. "What are you planning, Hunter?"

"We bring the entire village here to the castle. For one reason, they won't be fodder for those damn shifter monsters then. Another, they will be protected from anything else that might be thrown at them from the sorcerer. While they're here, Sloan and I will teach them self-defense methods. Knowing how to fight can't hurt, even if it's against a supernatural enemy." He rubbed a hand across his jaw. "Chances are the move is going to upset our sorcerer and it might even make him strike back in retaliation. Still, it might give us enough time for Briana to heal the Sphere. Everyone stands a better chance of survival if we're together, while we're waiting to see what's going to happen. Briana, you and Kassidy can put a spell on the perimeters of the castle, can't you? Something that might rebuke any spells against its defense."

"The castle is already guarded in that way," Kassidy told him. "But with Briana's help I can reinforce its strength." She rubbed at her head, her frown drawing her brows down in a sharp slant. "But, in order to take care of that many people under one roof, Briana and I will tax our own strength. If something was to suddenly happen, we might not have the power to help fight."

"Will it hurt you in any way?" Hunter asked, looking directly into Briana's eyes. He knew there wasn't any other option, but the thought that she would be in danger or hurt from using too much power, disturbed him deeply. His protective instincts where she was concerned were a bit on the extreme side, but he couldn't help it. He'd die protecting her if he had to.

"I don't know," she answered. Her gaze locked with his, and Hunter felt a jolt of desire hit him low in the stomach at her soft, confident words. "But, I know you'll do whatever you have to, to keep us safe."

Damn right he would. "Kassidy, are you well enough to go to the village? It's not going to be the best of organized moves, but the sooner we get everyone inside the castle, the better."

Two hours later the castle doors were sealed once again, with the entire village population inside its safe interior. Briana and Kassidy strengthened the protection spell, and Hunter could almost see the powerful aura surrounding the huge double doors. Could almost feel its power. As he worked with Sloan to organize everyone into groups, he couldn't help but think about how much he'd changed in the past days. Before he'd met Briana his whole world consisted of logic and normalcy. Before he'd even had the chance to accept the changes, one little witch had turned his world upside down and made him realize that not everything had to be so logical. Hell, if he was being honest with himself, he had to admit that he actually liked the change.

And all because one incredible woman had walked into his life and made him realize that she was—without a doubt—the center of his world. No matter what happened.

The truth shocked him.

And then he grinned.

He wouldn't change anything now. Not a damn thing. Just as long as she was with him. He may have to fight Hell itself to keep her safe, but he was determined that when all this was over, Briana Adair, a.k.a. enchanting witch, a.k.a. sexy siren, would be his.

Chapter Eighteen

The first round started close to midnight. Unbelievably fast. Inevitably deadly.

Briana was exhausted after helping Kassidy magically whip up meals for almost a hundred people, then later getting them all settled in rooms and anywhere else there was sleeping spaces. Blankets, pillows, cots, even baby cribs had to be magically created. Despite the hovering atmosphere of dread the adults had, the children were hyper and excited, and it took a few hours to finally calm them all down for sleep. Several had to be given sleeping potions.

Now, the castle lay sleeping, with the exception of Briana, Kassidy, Hunter, Sloan, and several men who had volunteered to sit in three of the tower rooms and watch for any approaching danger. The turret room housing the Sphere remained locked and secure.

Hunter and Sloan were set up in the great hall near the doors. Briana had made them cots but they weren't using them. Hunter paced the floor, deep in thought. And Sloan followed Kassidy on a round to make sure all the windows were properly guarded. Briana suspected it was because he just couldn't help aggravating the woman; something about her brought out Sloan's little boy side that made him want to see just how far he could go while pushing her buttons. Briana couldn't help but wonder how long it would take before Kassidy turned him into something.

She stood near the arched entrance to the great hall and watched Hunter pace for a few minutes. Her heart melted. He looked exhausted too. Yet, he kept going. He was an incredibly strong man, in more ways than one. She'd known that instantly about him when she'd first met him. Most humans would have freaked out when faced with something as supernatural as witchcraft. But not Hunter. First, he'd tried to disprove it. Then he'd accepted her for what she was. Now he was taking control of a situation that no human should ever have to face outside a nightmare, and his determination to win was keeping her ...

So sweetly agitated. With an insistent desire that just kept building, no matter what else was happening. *Face it*, she admitted with a sigh of acceptance, *he's the one you thought didn't exist. The man you never believed would come into your life. So, what are you going to do about it?*

Before she could think further on the dilemma, Hunter suddenly stopped pacing. She blinked fast, realizing he was standing right in front of her now. And staring at her like he could eat her up. *Oh Goddess.*

"You look tired, baby," he said, his tone caressingly husky. "Why don't you go to bed?"

Why did that simple question sound so—so sinfully tempting? Bed sounded nice. If he was there with her. She bit back another groan. Not the time or place. "Not any more tired than you, or the others are. Kassidy is confident the castle is warded strong enough. I don't think you need to stand guard."

Hunter grinned, looking way too devilish for the somber atmosphere around them. "Why don't we compromise? I'll settle down on the cot if you'll lie here with me."

"I'm not so sure that would be a smart idea," she told him, trying hard to hold back a smile. Not a smart idea, but Goddess did it ever sound good.

Hunter reached out and touched her cheek with a soft caress. His eyes darkened. "What harm could it do, sweetheart? It's not like I could ravish you with Sloan and Kassidy as an audience."

Her heart beat faster. "You're too comfortable with the idea of an audience as a protective buffer, Hunter. I'm not afraid you'll try anything either. It's just that—"

Hunter's caress slipped across her cheek until two of his fingers came to rest lightly on her lips. "That, what? That you're afraid lying in my arms would reveal your feelings for me?"

Was she that obvious? No sense in denying it now. "Maybe."

"We've had this connection since the first moment we met, Briana. I tried fighting it. Hell, maybe I should have tried harder but—"

What was he saying? Did he really mean that even though he was ready to admit he wanted her, he didn't like it? The thought hurt. Deeply. "I think you just insulted me. If you don't want to feel anything for me, then, that's fine." Not for anything would she let him see that hurt. "Just don't stand there acting as though you have no choice in the matter. I didn't put a love spell on you, or anything, if that's what you're worried about."

"I didn't say that, dammit. Stop twisting my words. And calm down. If you get upset Sloan is going to be ready and willing to come to your aid. And the way I'm feeling right now, I'd sooner beat the hell out of him than allow him to touch you."

"Stop being so condescending to me." How could one man make her feel so many different emotions at one time? She wanted to hate him for hurting her. She wanted to break his defenses and beg him to make love to her. She wanted to turn him into a slimy frog. Or ... turn him into the knight in shining armor she saw hidden beneath his tough façade. She just couldn't decide which route would be the best.

So she turned and walked away. Head high, strides fast. And with tears burning in her eyes. She knew part of it was because she was so exhausted. But her heart knew the real truth. She wanted Hunter to love her.

She was halfway up the first flight of stairs before he caught up with her. Grabbing her by the waist he spun her around and then effortlessly swung her up into his arms. His eyes were dark, hot, and he snared her gaze before she could hide her face against his shoulder.

"Where are you going, sweetheart?"

Darn it. He didn't have to sound so gentle, so caring. She wanted to stay mad at him. It was the only sane thing to do.

To her dismay the tears flooded her eyes. She sniffed and lowered her head against his shoulder. "My feet are cold," she muttered rebelliously. "I miss my bunny slippers."

Hunter chuckled, the sound sexy and sweet at the same time. "Sorry about that, honey. But," he growled sexily, his lips pressing against her bent head. "Absolutely no spell casting to transport them here. I'll warm your feet for you. Deal?"

She wanted to cuddle closer to him, feel his heat surround her. She wanted him to lose that darn calm façade and just give in to what was happening between them. But she stayed silent as he carried her back down the stairs and to the great hall. When he reached one of the cots, he put her down on the mattress, sat down, and pulled her feet into his lap. He slowly pulled off her soft slipper shoes, all the while keeping their gazes locked. His large warm hands enfolded her feet and he started rubbing gently. She leaned back against the wall behind her and willed her body to relax. But, oh Goddess, even a foot rub from this man was enough to set her on fire. If she'd been a cat, she would have purred. She couldn't stop her thoughts from straying to the erotic question of what else his hands could do to the rest of her body.

She didn't have to wait long to find out the answer. Tantalizingly slow, leaving a trail of hot caresses, Hunter moved both hands from her feet up to her ankles, then oh-so-slowly to her knees. Along the way his hands pushed her dress shift higher until it finally bunched around her upper thighs. He leaned over her now, his hands warm against the soft skin of her legs, his thumbs curled teasingly inward, close-but-not-close-enough to her center. Both their breathing escalated.

"Lean forward, baby," he said hoarsely. "Give me your lips while I touch you."

The moment their mouths met, Hunter moved his hand and covered her mound, his palm pressing against the silk of her panty. She moaned into his mouth, arching up to push back against his hand, and he rewarded her by slipping one finger inside the lining and rubbing across her nether lips. He made a growling sound deep in his throat and then shoved his finger in, straight to her clit. The rough possession was startling and Briana nearly came right then.

"Hot and wet," he muttered against her lips. He tapped against her, then rubbed hard. Inserting another finger, he moaned into her mouth, "Come for me, Briana. Do it now."

Sensation after sensation swamped her, instantly building to a hard and fast crescendo. She came. Hunter swallowed her soft cry with his hard lips, moaning his satisfaction. No sooner had her climax started to ease when he pulled his hands away, grabbed her hips and tugged hard and fast. She found herself lying flat, beneath him, and staring up into his dark, heated, gaze.

"I don't suppose you have a spell that would keep Sloan and

Kassidy occupied away from us, right now, do you?"

She grinned up at him. He looked so sexy, so aroused, yet so adorably frustrated at the same time. "Wish I did."

"Damn. So do I." He leaned down and kissed her, hard and quick. Breathing roughly he admitted in a near growl, "I'm dying here, Briana."

She was glad to know she wasn't the only one. "I feel like my entire insides are on fire."

Hunter groaned raggedly. "I want to be buried deep inside you right now, surrounded by all that sweet heat." He moved, settling heavier over her and then pushing his erection against her center. Briana groaned with the feel of him hot and hard against her.

But before she could respond, the sound of running feet on the marble floor echoed toward them. Hunter cursed out a few nasty expletives and then quickly sat up, pulling her up with him. He was just getting to his feet when one of the men from the towers skidded to a halt in front of them.

"Something is coming toward the castle," the man, Bruce, said as he tried hard to catch his breath between words. "At first it looked like a dark rolling mist on the ground. But as soon as it got closer I could see it looks like an army—or something else."

Briana's heart nearly stopped. Hunter had been right. It didn't take long for the sorcerer to discover they had moved everyone here. And she still hadn't figured out how to heal the Sphere. Without it to seal that door, the castle was the last place they wanted the Evil to be coming toward.

"Find Sloan and Kass," Hunter told her. "Meet me back here. I'll get the men." He instructed Bruce to get the other men in the towers. Briana ran from the great hall and toward the back of the castle where she'd last seen Sloan and Kassidy heading. As she ran, her thoughts flew in countless different directions. What were they going to do? How could they fight against a powerful sorcerer with only two witches, two trained men, and a handful of men who had no battle skills? Should she go to the tower room and try to heal the Sphere, in hopes it would only take a few precious minutes?

She nearly ran into Sloan and Kassidy coming from the kitchen. Sloan took one look at her and immediately pulled her into his arms, holding her against his chest for a long moment. He rubbed his hands up and down her back.

"We know. We saw them out the back window. They're coming from all angles up the hill. Calm down, honey. We're going to need you to be clear headed."

She knew he was right. She couldn't afford any necessary spells going awry because of chaotic emotions. Too much was at stake. Briana took a deep breath, exhaled, then moved out of his arms with a soft, "Thank you. Kass, what kind of army is it? Does the sorcerer have slaves or—followers?"

Kassidy's eyes were wide with her own unspoken fear. "I never realized he'd turned that many into those shifter beasts. He must have been gathering an army for a long while now."

Briana had to run to keep up with Sloan's fast strides back to the great hall. "Could you guess at how many, Sloan?"

"No," he ground out, "But I did notice they were well organized. They marched in unison, shoulder to shoulder, at least four per row."

Hunter had all the men waiting when they returned to the great hall. "Sweetheart," he touched her cheek with a soft caress. "I hate to do this to you and Kassidy, especially since you're still exhausted. But we're going to need weapons. Something accurate and deadly, but not complicated."

"We have to open the castle doors to use weapons," Kassidy spit out in anger. "How crazy is that?"

"Got a better idea?" Hunter frowned darkly at her. "Or would you rather them storm the place, break in, and kill everyone? My plan keeps the women and children safe inside."

Briana was wracking her brain for the perfect weapon, ignoring the heated argument between Hunter, Sloan, and Kassidy. What would work? Guns? No, there wasn't any time to train the men how to use them. Swords? No, that would be too dangerous. The thought of a group of untrained men swinging something long and sharp at anything that moved was a too-horrifying picture.

Maybe if she suited them with armor that was as impenetrable as possible? If the shifter beasts were simply mere creatures-once-men, then surely the other men would be able to fight fist to fist against them.

But she had to be sure. She had to know if the beasts were mere beasts—and not spelled into something supernaturally more powerful than the men they had been. Whatever spell she used on the defending men, she'd have to be sure it was as strong as the sorcerer had used on the others.

There was only one way to find out what she needed. Her heart rate sped up and she felt a little light-headed at the risk she'd be taking. She watched Hunter closely as she slowly backed away from him and the other two. All three were talking over the other, while the men grouped around them and offered their own opinions. She was able to back all the way out of the great hall completely unnoticed.

Inhaling a shaky breath she released it to utter the transportation spell. One moment she was safe inside the castle. The next moment she was walking behind the last shifter in a long line. Her knees nearly buckled; she was close enough to reach out and touch his back. It took everything she had in her to keep from screaming in complete fear.

Calm down, honey. She mentally repeated Sloan's constant mantra, over and over as she marched along behind the shifter beast. Over and over, until she realized she was either very calm right then—or insanely crazy and about to giggle uncontrollably at the absurdity of what she was about to do.

Before she could change her mind or lose any control over her emotions, she reached out and touched the shifter beast in front of her. "Excuse me," she said with a shaky grin, "Is this the way to the castle?"

The beast nearly tripped over his own feet as he squealed like the pig he resembled, jumped a foot in the air, and then swung around to face her. Instantly, Briana uttered the transportation spell again. Before her next breath, she and the shifter beast were transported to the small barn she had first arrived at. Luckily she was thinking clearly enough to land safely upright on the ground while at the same time spitting out a spell that automatically chained the beast to the wall.

She covered her ears with her hands as the beast squealed repeatedly and struggled to get free. "Stop that," she scolded above the ear-splitting shrieks. "I only borrowed you. It could have been worse. I could have killed you."

That comment did it. Immediately the beast stopped squealing. He stared at her as he panted heavily. Briana locked gazes with him, searching deep into his piggy eyes. Was the human still there, somewhere deep inside? Could she reverse the sorcerer's spell? Dare she try while she was still feeling exhausted ... not to mention still emotionally charged?

"Okay little piggy." She walked over to where he was, stopping a foot away. "Let's find out what else you can do besides eat people."

"Eat." The guttural voice made hard shivers race down her spine.

"Yes, I listed that. What else? Can you do everything your beast counterpart does? Or do you have other supernatural skills?"

"Eat."

"Wise guy. Get past that, please. You can't be that hungry; you're as fat as the proverbial pig."

"Eat. You."

"Okaaay. Not getting anywhere, really fast." She took a step closer. Outwardly she was as calm as she would ever be, and that's what she wanted him to see. But inside, she was shaking so hard it physically hurt. Nonetheless, she reached out and grasped a handful of the hair on his bare chest, then pulled. Hard.

He squealed. But he didn't—or couldn't retaliate. Just for good measure, Briana kicked him in the knee. He grimaced, growled, and then slobbered with fury, but still remained chained and unable to strike back. "Nothing? So, are you saying you're simply a flesh eating shifter beast under the spell of a sorcerer? Hmm. I think I can do something with that information."

"Eat. You. Now."

"Not in this lifetime, buddy." She searched her vast memory of spells and enchantments. There were several ways to turn something or someone into something else, but none she could think of to reverse a powerful sorcerer's personal shifting spell.

She felt a moment of panic again. Even as powerful a witch as Kassidy was—and she had to be in order to have 'borrowed' the Sphere in the first place—she was still afraid of this sorcerer and doubted that they had the power or skills to fight him. That didn't bode well. If they didn't find a way to fight back—and win—then the consequences would be beyond disastrous.

But ... if I heal the Sphere then it's possible the sorcerer will be defeated. If that door is permanently sealed, he wouldn't stay here. She'd take the Sphere back to her world, safe guard it with every ounce of witch strength she had in her, and hope nothing this crazy ever happened again. *Ha. Happy ever after? Why do I have this feeling that's not a possibility?*

"Eat. You. Now. Now."

"Oh," She managed to grin at the disgruntled beast. "Didn't I mention that witches taste horrible? You'd get heartburn for sure. So I'm being really nice by preventing you from eating me." She studied him for a few minutes. Should she leave him here or try and reverse the spell? No, she didn't have the time or the energy to spare. He'd have to stay chained until the battle was over. Just to be on the safe side, she spell cast the chains with more binding strength. "Relax awhile, piggy. Your comrades will have to fight without you. I'll come back later and tell you how the war turned out." She transported, hearing his squeals of rage echoing in her ears.

Unfortunately for her, she landed at Hunter's feet.

"Uh oh."

Chapter Nineteen

"**O**h yeah," Hunter muttered as he stared down at her with a glare so angry she felt decidedly singed. "Be afraid, little witch. Be very afraid." He reached down and grabbed her by the waist then hauled her to her feet. She lost her balance and fell against his hard, unyielding chest. Their faces were a mere inch apart. "I don't know whether to shake you to death or turn you over my knees," he told her. "Where the hell did you disappear to? Damn it, Briana, I almost had a heart attack when I realized you were gone."

"Um, I had an idea." Yeah, that sounded reasonable enough. Or not. His features darkened even more and she chewed on her bottom lip, hesitant to tell the rest.

"Care to share?"

"Only if you release me first, and let Sloan stand in front of me."

Hunter groaned, disgust and frustration clear. "Then, which one of you do you want me to punish first," he demanded on a low sexy growl. "You for pulling another crazy stunt, or Sloan for daring to be your choice of protector?"

"You're not being reasonable, Hunter."

"Baby, reason and logic flew right out the window when you came into my life."

"You don't have to sound like that's a bad thing," she told him, hoping to stall until she could get a few feet away from him.

"It's open for debate," he muttered, "But not right now. Where did you disappear to, Briana?"

"Information mission."

"Hear that sound?" Hunter scowled. "That's my patience snapping its last line."

"Okay!" She pushed against his chest and managed to break away. She took a few steps back and bumped into Sloan.

"Sorry, honey," Sloan told her as he stopped her escape. "I'm siding with Hunter on this. Now isn't the time to be doing anything crazy."

Briana gave up. Either way, someone was going to be angry. Hunter, because he was so overly protective of her. Sloan, because he was her buffer. Kassidy, because she hadn't shared her plan with her first. She took a deep breath then answered in a hyper rush, "I transported outside to the army. I kidnapped one of the shifter beasts, transported us to the barn, chained him to a wall, then interrogated him to see what kind of powers he might have."

Hunter stared at her like she'd suddenly gone crazy. His handsome face was flushed with anger, but his eyes were dark with some other emotion. He opened his mouth and then shut it again. Running a hand over his face, he abruptly turned and stomped away.

"God, Briana, that was a stupid thing to do." Sloan swung her around to face him. "Are you that naïve to think that kind of stunt would be safe? The damn beast could have killed you."

Anger surged from deep inside her. She was getting tired of Hunter and Sloan's condescending attitudes. "I'm not stupid, Sloan. I made sure he was securely chained. And it wasn't a crazy stunt. We needed to know just how strong these beasts are, and what kind of powers they may have."

"And what did you find out?" Hunter had come back to stand beside her. She searched his face and her heart stuttered. His features, like his voice, were void of any telling emotions. She swallowed a sad sigh. She'd rather face his anger head on, instead of this too quiet composure.

"Apparently they're just enchanted," she answered. "I tested him and he wasn't able to counterattack."

Kassidy spoke for the first time since she'd returned. "You didn't sense any other power aura around him?"

Briana shook her head. "So, that means they can be defeated. If we can just figure out how."

Kassidy frowned. "I tried to break the enchantment spell and couldn't. And, I tried to kill them with magic. I don't know what else to do."

"Maybe your magic is ineffective against them," Hunter stated, and Briana clearly heard the reluctance in his voice. "There's the possibility that Briana's will work differently because she's not from here."

Surprised that he would concur that so easily, Briana stared at him. "I can transport back to the barn and try a spell on the beast."

Hunter grunted and frowned hard at her. "You've already used a lot of magic, and you're exhausted. It will have to wait. Kassidy says that the castle walls can't be breached with anything those beasts have for now, so we keep them locked out and stall for time. You both need to rest. Do it now, while we still have that time." He nodded to Sloan. "We need to get these men whipped into fighting shape as soon as possible. Those damn beasts may not have a weapon to break inside with, but as soon as that sorcerer shows up, all bets are off." Without even looking at her again, he turned and walked away. Briana stared at his retreating back, her heart feeling heavy. Had her little side trip done irreparable damage to their tentative relationship?

Kassidy touched her arm. "He was frightened for you, when he discovered you had disappeared. You can't blame him for being angry. Your man and his brother seem to have an overabundance of the protective gene."

Briana sighed. "I had to do something."

Kassidy smiled, looped her arm through hers and led her out of the great hall. "If he truly cares about you, he will not stay angry long. And he's right. We do need to restore our energy."

Briana stopped at the foot of the stairs and stared up. "I need to try to heal the Sphere again."

"If you try without regaining your energy, it could kill you. And I refuse to have to face your man and tell him I allowed you to do that. Come, we'll go to the Library and rest there."

It wasn't easy. She tossed and turned on the small cot, her thoughts and emotions so chaotic she couldn't settle down. And the silence was deafening. When they had looked out the Library window they saw the army of shifter beasts just standing outside, still, and waiting. That oddly patient waiting stance was grating on her nerves.

Because she knew why they were simply waiting. The sorcerer

was coming.

Then, Goddess help them.

Two hours later the battle began in earnest. He had arrived.

As one unbreakable force the shifter beasts surged toward the castle. Those inside, standing at windows, wondered what the beasts planned since not one of them carried any weapons. But when the mass slammed into the castle exterior, the walls shook.

Kassidy turned a shade paler and winced as the aftershock reverberated beneath their feet. "The sorcerer must have used a battering spell."

"Will the walls, windows and the doors hold?" Hunter demanded. He had men posted at every window on the first floor, and a large group guarding the front doors. Briana and Kassidy had conjured up weapons—swords, much to Briana's dismay—and each man was armed with smaller knives as well. They had magically blessed the weapons to pierce any substance, and Briana could only hope they wouldn't be tearing through human skin.

Kassidy shook her head at Hunter's question. "I'm not sure anymore. I thought I had this castle well protected with my spells, but—"

"Not the time to fall apart on us, witch," Sloan told her when she paused and closed her eyes tight for a long moment. "We need you both to be at your strongest."

Kassidy glared at him. But she took a deep fortifying breath, released it, and then turned to Briana. "We'll need to reinforce the warding on the windows and doors."

She went in one direction and Briana in the other. Outside, the wave of beasts hit the castle walls again and even the floor trembled. Briana's heart raced as she hurried from one window to the next and quickly strengthened the warding spells. If those beasts managed to get in, there was no telling what the outcome would be. The villagers weren't trained warriors, and there were so few of them compared to the beasts' numbers outside. Chances were that they would all be slaughtered in a matter of minutes.

She couldn't let that happen. Somewhere outside, waiting for his minions to do the grunt work and get him inside was an enemy that had to be stopped—no matter the cost. And the only way to stop him from reaching his goal was to permanently close that door in the basement.

She had to heal the Sphere.

And in order to get past the mysterious repelling spell on the room where the Sphere rested, she would need a serious—and no doubt dangerous—distraction. The sorcerer couldn't be alerted to what she was doing.

She and Kassidy returned to the main hall where Hunter and Sloan waited with the others. Her gut was tied in knots, knowing that Hunter was going to explode when she told him her plan. The only solution was to tell him quick and then do it—before he had the chance to stop her.

"As long as the sorcerer is concentrating on the door here, he's able to keep the repelling spell on the room where the Sphere is," she stated, avoiding Hunter's direct stare. "We need to distract him from the castle. He knows I'm here. So, I'm going to transport outside. Right in front of him. And then I'm going to lead him on a merry chase before I transport back."

"No way in hell." Hunter's scowl was so dark and his tone so deadly she cringed. "Think again. You so much as start to disappear and I'll have you locked in my arms so fast you won't be able to take your next breath."

Briana took a cautious step back from him. He followed, moving up against her so fast she didn't have time to blink. "Hunter, this is the only solution. We have to distract him."

"It's suicidal," Kassidy told her, fear in her tone. "He'll catch you."

Hunter clasped her upper arms in a tight, painful grip. "I'm not going to allow you to do this, Briana." He shook her slightly. "We'll think of something else."

"Like what?" she demanded. Why couldn't he see this was the only way? Time was running out for them. Even now the floor trembled from another onslaught of the castle walls. This time the hit was so hard she might have lost her balance and fallen if Hunter hadn't been holding her. As it was, Kassidy fell against Sloan, with a little shriek right in his ear. Sloan rubbed his ear and muttered, "Damn witches that can't stay calm," but nonetheless righted her and pulled her close to his side.

Briana and Hunter stared into each other's eyes. She saw mixed emotions swirling in the dark blue grey depths, his anger, his worry, his protectiveness. And deeper still, she saw something else that made her heart stutter. She so wanted the time to tell him she felt the same way about him. What if they never got that chance? What if everything ended here, now?

"He doesn't know what you look like."

Briana blinked rapidly to clear her muddled thoughts and raised her brow in response to Hunter's sudden statement. "Why would that matter?"

"He only knows that a powerful witch has come from a parallel world. Witches can be female or male, right?"

"Yes." She wasn't sure she liked where this seemed to be leading.

"You can do glamour spells, right?"

Briana's heart nearly stopped. She shook her head. "No. Don't even suggest it, Hunter. Please."

"Sorry, baby." He pulled her closer. Briana wanted to snuggle into his arms and beg him to never let her go. "It's the only way this little plan of yours is going to happen. I'll go in your place. With enough of a glamour spell on me, he's sure to think I'm the witch he needs to worry about."

"But, I'd have to be with you to transport you back." Her mind was racing, trying to come up with a good argument. "Or you would have to keep running while I stayed here and tried to heal the Sphere. We can't risk that, Hunter. He could try a spell against you, or he could even catch you. No, I can't even think about it."

"I'd rather you did the glamour spell and the transporting, Briana," Hunter told her, his voice firm. "But if you won't, then Kassidy will. She can transport me there and back."

"I will not." Kassidy stepped away from Sloan. "The plan is no crazier with you doing it than it was with Briana doing it."

"You will do it." Sloan grabbed her by the arm and hauled her up against him again. "You'll help Briana do the spell. On Hunter. And me." He looked at his brother. "Two are better than one, bro."

Hunter nodded his head. He leaned in and kissed Briana lightly on the lips. "No more arguments. Let's get this done."

She definitely wanted to argue. She wanted to rage at his darn macho attitude. She wanted to hold onto him and never let go. She let her head drop to his chest for a long moment while he held her closer and murmured softly in her ear. "It will be all right, Briana, I promise."

"You had better stay safe, Hunter," she threatened on a catchy breath, "Or I swear I'll never forgive you."

"Hey," he whispered sexily, "Why don't you give me a kiss and remind me what I'll be coming back to."

Briana lifted her head and met his mouth descending to hers. She put everything in that kiss. All her feelings for this incredible man. All the love she felt. All the desire.

And Hunter gave it all back. She felt it to the very depths of her soul.

One of the men on guard in one of the towers was able to tell them where the sorcerer was amidst the army of shifter beasts. "He's in the very back, on the west side. There are several heavily armored beasts circling him. He's very tall, standing above all the others, and wearing a long black cape."

Still expressing their trepidation, Briana and Kassidy clasped hands and began the chant for the glamour spell. It would make the two men appear as though their auras were magical, and powerful, and thus fool the sorcerer into thinking they were the witches. Bright, multi colors swirled around them, clinging like a second skin. When that was done, the two women uttered the words that would send Hunter and Sloan out of the castle and directly into the path of the sorcerer. Kassidy, along with two others, would watch from the tower as the two men led the sorcerer away. They would be able to keep track and know when it was time to cast the spell to bring them back. Briana would go to the tower room and heal the Sphere.

"Please, Goddess," she whispered as she watched Hunter fade from her sight, "Keep them safe. Bring him back to me." In all her life, she'd never felt the utter helplessness and heartache as she did then.

She didn't bother walking. As soon as the men disappeared, she transported to the tower room. She would know as soon as the sorcerer was distracted and directed his power elsewhere. She stood outside the door, her whole body shaking, and tried hard to stay calm. The last thing Sloan had said to her was "Stay calm, honey. Don't make me have to come back too soon, just so you can cling to me for support. Hunter is about ready to kill me just for letting you think about doing that."

With a calming intake of air, she smiled. Sloan had purposely teased her, knowing her thoughts would be chaotic. She would make him proud, no matter how hard her body was shaking and her nerves were screaming with doubts and fear. She wouldn't fail them.

In the blink of an eye, the strange black aura hovering over the surface of the door disappeared. She knew it had to mean that Hunter and Sloan were now distracting the sorcerer. He was powerful, but not enough to expand his powers inside and still use them to chase after what he assumed was another powerful witch. If he thought the witch who could heal the Sphere was fleeing away from the castle, then his thoughts and powers didn't need to be exclusively directed there.

Briana pushed open the door and rushed inside to where the Sphere still sat on the pedestal. She came to a skidding halt, crying out with a choked sob. "Oh, Goddess!" Looking small, pale and wilted, the Tree was nearly dead! Her hands shook as she picked up the Sphere and she clutched it to her heart.

Ancient words from deep within her, surfaced. The Life-Giving words for the Living Willow Tree flowed from her mouth as though they were visible letters floating in the air. She called upon the long-reaching, undying power of all her ancestors, all those who had served and protected the Sphere over the centuries. She dug deep inside herself and pulled forth every ounce of energy and life giving support she possessed. She spoke the healing words with heartfelt, soul-felt conviction that they would be obeyed.

A blinding burst of multi colors lit the entire room the same time a ferocious force of wind swirled like a mini tornado and sent the colors spinning crazily like a huge kaleidoscope display. A power unlike any she had ever felt, or knew existed, burst from somewhere deep inside her and left her body with a swoosh that matched the sound of a loud chorus of chanting voices.

Dazed, bereft of any life-giving energy, Briana looked down at the Sphere in her shaking hands. She had one brief moment to feel indescribable joy at the sight of the strong, standing tall, Living Willow Tree.

Then, a blackness that had no bottom filled her vision, stole what strength she had left, and she felt herself falling. Falling into a place she wasn't sure she would ever be able to return from.

Chapter Twenty

Shaking off the dizziness Hunter grumbled, "I'll never get used to this damn teleporting deal."

Sloan spit out an expletive along with the mouthful of grass. "At least you always end up standing. Both times I've been face down. I'm beginning to think it's done on purpose."

Both men took a minute to assess their location. They had landed in a cluster of thick bushes just right for concealment behind the army stationed in front of the castle. It only took a moment to locate the sorcerer. He stood off to the side, tall and imposing, his black aura visible even from the short distance. His long, black cloak effectively concealed his shape, and the large cowl kept his features hidden.

"What's the plan, bro?"

Hunter ran a thorough gaze over the army mass. "He has approximately one hundred men. At least that balances the scales if they manage to get into the castle." He didn't want to think about that possibility. It was taking a lot of willpower not to think about Briana and what might be happening even now as she tried to heal the Sphere. He needed to be there to protect her. He resolutely pushed the trepidation away. Right now was the priority. "One of us has to get close enough to get his attention—and his alone. Then lead him back into the forest here. We'll split up and head in two different directions. We'll make a run for it and hope he follows one of us. Do you remember the location of the barn from here? Kassidy knows we'll head there for her to retrieve us."

"And if he catches us?" Sloan frowned darkly. "Why didn't we think to ask Briana to conjure our guns?"

Hunter shook his head. "Our luck they wouldn't have worked

here. We're both good runners, Sloan. We can manage to keep ahead of him as long as he doesn't get us in his spell-casting range." How much time would Briana need? Could they stay out of the sorcerer's range long enough for her to do what she had to do? *Stay safe, sweetheart. And hurry.*

Hunter chose to be the one to approach the sorcerer. All his prior training of using stealth and quiet, undetected moves came into play as he cautiously made his way to where the sorcerer stood. When he was a few yards away he stopped. *Damn, the evil stench off this bastard is potent enough to make a skunk run the other way.* He swallowed the bile that rose in his throat. There wasn't any doubt that this man was far more evil than any other he'd ever come across in his career. How did you fight something like that?

He braced his body in preparation of any spell strike and then cleared his throat purposely loud. "Hey, man. Busy?" Just as he'd expected the sorcerer jumped and then swung around to face him. Hunter got a glimpse of his face under the covering cowl. Monster didn't do him justice.

The sorcerer raised his hands toward Hunter but paused. His rough voice sounded hoarse and grating. "Who are you? Are you the witch from the parallel world? Or one of her apprentices?"

Hunter shot him a look of disdain. "I'm the one, buddy. Mind telling me why you're trying to attack my friend's castle?" *Always keep the enemy off guard.*

Eyes glowed eerily red, deep within the cowl. "Don't bother playing innocent with me. We both know why you are here in this world. You want the Sphere." A growling laugh came from his mouth, oddly echoing. "Having trouble getting to it?"

Hunter kept his expression neutral. Hopefully, the answer to that question was a definite no. How much more time did Briana need?

He didn't need to wait for an answer. The sorcerer suddenly jerked as though he'd been struck. His head shot up and he spun around to face the castle. "No!"

Hunter knew Briana had reached the Sphere. Maybe she'd healed it already. It was his cue. He took off in a fast sprint back into the forest. Over his shoulder he yelled the taunt, "Follow me, you bastard, if you want it back."

The roar that echoed behind him would have felled even

the bravest man. As it was, Hunter almost lost his footing. He straightened and pushed his speed up another notch. As he flew deeper into the forest he saw a flash of Sloan as he ran parallel to him, twisting in and out of the trees. They would stay visible until the sorcerer got too close, then split. Heavy footsteps behind him and angry, bellowing roars of rage ate up the distance between them and Hunter pushed his body into a faster run.

He knew the instant the sorcerer saw Sloan, too. The threatening roar shook the ground beneath his feet. Without warning, something crashed next to Hunter as he sprinted through a set of tall trees. He barely had time to register that it was a lightning bolt hitting the tree closest to him. Another bolt hit at his heels as he surged forward. He felt the electricity shiver over his skin, and cussed. *What's next? Hellfire?*

He shouldn't have even thought it. A huge blast of fire hit the ground in front of him. Hunter skidded to a halt stopping in time to keep from plowing straight into it. The trees immediately caught fire, going up in ferocious, towering flames and effectively caging him in. Hunter's heart lurched. He looked to the side and saw Sloan in the same precarious position. The sorcerer had them both cornered. Damn, he hadn't expected this move. What the hell were they going to do?

Just as the scorching flames crept closer, Hunter felt the now familiar dizziness that accompanied teleporting. Seconds later he was lying on the floor of the castle's hallway and panting for much needed air. Beside him Sloan choked out a smoky cough. "Hell. That was cutting it a bit close, witch."

Kassidy snorted unladylike and ignored Sloan as she looked at Hunter. "Briana has healed the Sphere. She's on her way to the cellar now to permanently close the door. We've got to join her, before the sorcerer realizes what's going on."

Hunter didn't stop to ask questions. He made a dash to the cellar. There, he skidded to a halt and saw Briana standing in the middle of the circle over the door's entranceway. Their gazes collided. His heart nearly stopped, his breath catching in his chest. Her beautiful emerald eyes shone with an inner power that blazed with unearthly green fire. Her entire body glowed with an incredibly ethereal beauty, as though she was some unworldly fey being.

For one long heart-stopping moment Hunter had the deep gut

feeling that he had lost her. His chance to claim her as his own was gone. She was beyond him now. And the realization hurt deeper than anything ever had in his entire life. He felt a part of his soul die.

Chapter Twenty+One

Briana's heart swelled with joy at seeing Hunter there and safe. It took every ounce of willpower she had to keep from running straight into his arms. But she had to stay where she was. The Sphere was pulsing with its magical energy and otherworldly power, radiating through her body like a conduit as it forced a permanent seal over the door and closed the portal's leak. The amazingly pleasurable streaks of electricity pulsing through her from the Sphere were exhilarating. She had to keep forcing air into her lungs just to breathe.

She knew the exact moment the Sphere had finished its spell. All the air rushed from her and she felt enveloping, suffocating fatigue swamp over her and through her. She felt herself falling. She hit the floor before Hunter could reach her. Stunned, impossibly weak, she whispered his name as she felt his strong arms lift her.

"Briana," Hunter choked out a hoarse groan. "Open your eyes and tell me you're all right. Now, sweetheart, before I die of fear."

"Dramatic, aren't you?" Kassidy knelt down beside them. "She's fine. Give her a moment to catch her breath. And Sloan, if you give me that nasty glare one more time I'm going to retaliate. Back off, now."

Briana managed a smile. She opened her eyes to stare into Hunter's. "Hi."

Hunter grinned. "Hi. Is Kassidy right? You're fine?"

She nodded. The debilitating fatigue was slowly fading. Her entire body was infused with the deep, soul-felt joy that the Sphere had closed the door, and they had won. She suddenly shivered. Or had they won, completely? "What about the sorcerer? What happened?"

Just as she finished speaking the floor beneath them shook and rolled, almost buckling. The walls shook hard, and they could hear windows breaking upstairs. It wasn't over yet. Women screaming, children crying, and men shouting, reached them. Hunter carefully helped Briana to her feet and they followed a running Kassidy and Sloan out of the cellar. The floors and walls continued to shake and they had a hard time keeping their balance. Along the hallway, they had to dodge falling objects, pictures, and falling chunks of crumbling walls.

In the great hall they found the men crowded around the big oak doors. One man spotted Hunter and shouted, "They're breaking down the doors!"

Kassidy threw a strengthening spell on the doors a moment too late. The wide doors crashed open, throwing men in all directions. Hunter and Sloan rushed into the foray as the wave of shifter monsters came flooding in. Battle cries roared above the deafening chaos. Swords sliced through air and skin, and animalistic growls and roars clashed with the horrific sounds of the wounded and dying. Briana and Kassidy stood at the back of the hall and threw spells, trying to kill as many of the shifter monsters as they could hit. But it wasn't easy. The great hall was too crowded with both enemy and defenders and it was almost impossible to separate one from the other.

And the more spells she threw, the weaker Briana became. Her body wasn't fully recovered from using the Sphere, but she couldn't just stand there and not help. She knew she had to do something more. But what? Frantic, she tried to keep Hunter and Sloan in her sight but there was just too much chaos. If she threw a destruction spell on the entire group, even the good guys would die. And if something happened to Hunter ... then she would die too. She knew that with a soul-deep conviction.

A resounding boom crashed over the horrific sounds of battle. Briana choked back a scream of fear as she looked up and saw the sorcerer step inside. Goddess, this couldn't end well no matter what she tried!

He towered above all the others, black from head to toes, evil stench and immense power wafting off him and around him like a visible flow of grey smoke. And those glowing red eyes of his sought and then caught her gaze. She felt his punch of evil power like a physical blow. He knew who she was—and he knew she was holding the Sphere.

The Sphere was in her dress pocket and she held it tight in her hand. She squared her shoulders and braced her body. She would willingly die before she allowed him to get to the Sphere. It had all come down to this now.

Kassidy rushed to her side. Her voice was hoarse, her face extremely pale. "What can we do?"

There was only one thing she could do. And Briana knew it meant she would have to sacrifice her life to accomplish it. Because if she used that much power, her body wouldn't survive the drastic drain of life-giving energy. She was too weak as it was.

But wasn't that what being the Guardian of the Sphere meant? Her sacrifice for the sake of the world?

Deep within, to the very center of her soul, she knew she had to do this. A soul-touching calm settled over her, blocking out the battle, the fear, the knowledge of what she would lose.

"Kassidy, there's only one thing left to try. I will have to use my power to transport the sorcerer somewhere and then use the Sphere to bind him permanently there as a prisoner."

Kassidy gasped, her features paling more. "You can't! It will kill you to use that kind of power!"

Even though only mere moments had passed since the sorcerer had entered, Briana knew there was no time left. "You have to promise me something," she said hurriedly. "Promise me you will send Hunter and Sloan back to their world. Promise me, Kassidy!"

"Yes," Kassidy answered, still shaking her head, "but this is crazy, Briana. Please don't try it. We'll combine our powers. Maybe we can defeat him that way."

"No," Briana stressed, "You will need your powers to heal after this battle is over. I'm betting the shifter monsters will disappear as soon as the sorcerer is bound. He created them, but once his range of power is completely contained, he can't keep them manifested." She took a deep breath, then exhaled slowly, willing her heart to stop beating so fast. Wishing the pain wasn't so hard to bear. "One last promise, Kassidy, please. Tell Hunter ... tell him that I loved him."

She didn't hesitate another moment. She pulled the Sphere from her pocket and raised it high to be sure the sorcerer was looking directly at it. With all the strength she had left, with all the immense power she had within her, she shouted the words to the spell that would damn them both to a fate nothing could change ever again.

> *Powers that be, hear me now.*
> *Bring forth the strength of the Union that binds us,*
> *Know my Spell and embrace it,*
> *Send all the ancestors' power behind it.*
> *Cleave to me, this sorcerer be,*
> *Take us where Prison awaits the Evil that is he.*

A horrific roar of rage reached her ears just as the Sphere flashed out a blinding streak of light and she felt the room disappear around her. But the last thing she heard would haunt her for whatever time she had left to live.

Hunter's cry of her name.

Chapter Twenty+Two

Although two months passed and life continued without change, Hunter still couldn't bring himself to leave Inverness and return back to his old life and job. He finally resigned and then took a job as detective with the same police department Sloan worked for. His work kept him sane and he stayed immersed in it for long hours every day, well into the late hours of night, until he'd drag him self home in complete exhaustion.

Exhaustion kept him from remembering. Most of the time. But it was nights like tonight that he couldn't do anything else but remember. If he'd been a drinker, he'd willingly be knee deep in a liquor stupor all the time just to try and drown the pain.

Now, just like too many other nights, he found himself lying in bed staring up at the ceiling. His mind played over that last scene with Kassidy at the castle. Her stark, destructive words kept echoing in his head.

"She knew it was the only solution, Hunter. You have to accept that. If she hadn't done this, we would all be dead now."

As opposed to her being dead now? He couldn't accept it. Kassidy had then told him she would send him and Sloan back to their own world, but he had refused. He wasn't going anywhere without Briana, and he refused to believe she was dead. It was obvious that somehow she had managed to contain the sorcerer, that her plan to imprison him must have worked, because right in the middle of the battle all the shifter monsters had suddenly disintegrated into nothing but piles of fur bits and bones scattered across the bloodied floor. But he wasn't about to leave without Briana, and he was determined to find her.

After days of relentlessly searching, he still wasn't ready to admit defeat. He couldn't. But Kassidy finally faced off with him and told him that she would honor Briana's request despite his refusal to give up. One minute Hunter had been yelling at her, and the next minute he and Sloan were standing in his mother's backyard.

The pain and loss nearly killed him.

He'd lost the love of his life, the other half of his soul, before he'd even had the chance to claim her. How the hell he was going to live with that wasn't something he wanted to dwell on. Common sense told him that he had to go on living. He didn't have to like it, but he didn't have a choice.

Despite his painful thoughts, Hunter finally drifted off into a restless sleep. In his dreams, he hunted for the sexy witch that had stolen his heart and soul. But he never found her.

"Ooomph!" The choked exclamation brought Hunter out of his sleep. In one split second his self defense kicked in and he started to strike out. In the next heart-stopping second his befuddled mind registered the fact that the warm body lying across him was completely naked.

"Briana!"

"Ouch, Hunter! You yelled into my ear!"

Hunter threw his arms around her and sat up, shifting her to his lap. "To hell with your poor ear," he exclaimed, his voice husky despite the shock. "Are you really here? This isn't a dream?"

She pinched him on the arm. "Are you doubting me again? I swear, Hunter, I thought we were past that disbelieving stage."

"I'm going to strangle you," he threatened silkily, "If you don't start talking—fast—and tell me what's going on? My God, Briana, I thought you were dead!"

Briana settled against his chest and looked up into his face. Her smile was so sweet, so beautiful, that he lost his breath again. To hell with explanations. He was going to kiss her senseless.

She stopped him just as his lips were about to touch hers. "First, I explain, then we kiss."

Hunter grinned wickedly. "Kissing is only the beginning. I told you that the next time you ended up on top of me, deliciously naked, I wasn't going to stop. So, talk fast, baby. Real fast."

He watched her lovely features turn somber. He pushed back the fear that he wouldn't like what she was about to say. But it didn't matter. He had her now and no way in hell was he ever letting her go.

"I almost died," Briana said quietly. "But I had to do it, Hunter. I transported the sorcerer to that barn. Then, with what strength and power I had left, I spell cast the building to become a permanent prison for him. It worked. The Sphere closed the doors and sealed them for eternity. But the spell nearly destroyed me. I can't explain what exactly happened after that, or where I was; you wouldn't understand. Their healing almost didn't work. I lay in a dark place for a long time, hovering between life and death—and not caring anymore. But their combined powers finally worked to heal me completely, and then they sent me back to the castle. Kassidy sent me home."

Hunter shook his head, his mind and heart so full he couldn't speak for a long time. He tightened his arms around her. She was here, real, warm, and … his.

"Maybe you'll explain it all to me one day," he told her softly, "but for now it doesn't matter. Whoever 'they' are, I'm eternally grateful to them."

Briana searched his eyes and he stared back knowing that all the love he felt for this woman was there for her to clearly see.

"Where do we go from here, Hunter?" Her tone sounded vulnerable and it touched him deep.

"I'm thinking we can skip the kissing and go directly to the making love part," he told her, moving his arms over her back in a firm caress.

"And after?"

"Do it again." Hunter touched her lips softly with his. "And again. And again."

Briana sat up straighter and tried to pull back but he tightened his grip. She frowned at him. "Are you just going to avoid the real issue here?"

Hunter knew what she was referring to. Their feelings for each other had happened fast and furious, and all that had occurred afterward hadn't left them time to accept their feelings or figure out what to do about them.

"What do you want to do, Briana?" He almost held his breath, waiting for her answer.

"I'm still a witch, that hasn't changed. I still have hiccups with my spells when my emotions are involved. I'm still Guardian of the

Sphere—for the rest of my life. I'm nowhere close to being a normal woman; as you can attest to, I can easily cause chaos without much effort. What man in his right mind would want a woman like me to—stay around?"

"My turn," he murmured. "I'm stubborn to extreme measures. I don't like losing. I prefer logic to illogical explanations. I can't wield a sword good enough to chop off the head of a monster; I'll have to learn. Maybe. So, why would a sexy siren of a witch want that kind of man?"

"I do."

The words were murmured in a sweetly soft, heartfelt, soulful whisper. But it sealed their fate forever. Because they both said it at the same time.

Kari Thomas

Kari Thomas has been writing for years. An active member of RWA's Desert Rose and Northern Arizona chapters, this multi-published author is a bookaholic with over 3,000 titles in her collection. She loves to research subjects like history, religions and the supernatural. Raised in Florida, Thomas moved to Arizona in her teen years, and still resides there.

www.AuthorKari.com